SPECIAL DELIVERY

Also by Danielle Steel

DANIELLE STEEL

SPECIAL DELIVERY

Delacorte  Press

Published by
Delacorte Press
Bantam Doubleday Dell Publishing Group, Inc.
1540 Broadway
New York, New York 10036

Library of Congress Cataloging in Publication Data
Steel, Danielle.
    Special delivery / Danielle Steel.
        p.   cm.
    ISBN 0-385-31691-7
    I. Title.
PS3569.T33828S67   1997
813'.54—dc21   97-5349
                                        CIP

Manufactured in the United States of America
Published simultaneously in Canada

July 1997

10 9 8 7 6 5 4 3 2 1

BVG

To Tom,
For all the happy times,
with all my love,
d.s.

Chapter One

The tires of the red Ferrari squealed, as it came around the corner and dove neatly into the space where Jack Watson always parked it. It was in the parking lot of his Beverly Hills store, Julie's. Exactly twenty years before, he had named it after his then nine-year-old daughter. It had been a lark to him then, something he was going to do for fun, after deciding to give up producing movies.

He had produced seven or eight low-budget films, none of them remarkable, and before that he had spent half a dozen years, after college, working on and off as an actor. His film career had been relatively minor, filled with all the usual hope and promises that never turned out quite as he planned, and too often turned out to be disappointing. But his

luck changed when he got into retail with the unex-
pected help of an uncle, who had left him some
money. Without even trying, it seemed, he wound
up with the store that every woman in Los Angeles
would have killed to shop in. His wife helped him
with the buying at first, but within two years he figured out that he had a better eye for the merchandise
than she did. And much to her chagrin, also for the
women who wore it. Every woman in town, actresses
and socialites, models and just ordinary housewives
with money to spend, wanted to go to Julie's . . .
and meet Jack Watson. He was one of those men
who didn't even have to try. Women were just drawn
to him like bees to honey. And he loved it. And
them.

Two years after he opened his store, to no one's
surprise but his own, his wife left him. And for the
past eighteen years, he had to admit, he had never
missed her. He had met her on the set of one of his
films, she had come to read for him, and spent the
next two weeks lost in passion with him in his
Malibu cottage. He had been madly in love with her
at first, and they were married six months later, his
first and only foray into marriage. It had lasted for
fifteen years and two kids, but had ended with all the
bitterness and venom that, as far as he was concerned, was inevitable in any marriage. He had only
been tempted to try it again once in the years afterward, with a woman who was far too smart to have

him. She was the only woman who had ever made him want to be faithful to her, and for once he had been. He had been in his forties then, she had been thirty-nine, French, and a very successful artist. They had lived together for two years, and when she died in an accident on her way to meet him in Palm Springs, he had thought he would never recover from it. For the first time in his life, Jack Watson had known real pain. She was everything he had always dreamed of, and in rare moments of seriousness even now, he still said she was the only woman he had ever loved, and he meant it. Dorianne Matthieu was funny and irreverent, sexy and beautiful, and in her own way, utterly outrageous. She didn't put up with anything from him, and she said that only a fool would marry him, but he had never doubted for a moment that she loved him. And he adored her. She took him to Paris to meet her friends, and they had traveled everywhere together, Europe, Asia, Africa, South America. To him, it had always seemed that the moments he spent with her were tinged with magic. Until she died and left him with the resounding emptiness and overwhelming sense of loss that he actually thought might kill him.

There had been women since, lots of them, to fill the nights and the days. In the dozen years since her death, he had hardly ever been alone, not physically anyway, but he had never loved another woman either, nor did he want to. As far as he was concerned, loving was far too painful. At fifty-nine, Jack Watson had everything he had ever wanted: a business that seemed to do nothing but grow and crank out money.

He had opened a Palm Springs store, before Dori died, and another in New York five years later. And for the past two years, he had been thinking about opening one in San Francisco. But at his age, he was no longer entirely sure he wanted the headaches of further expansion. Maybe if his son, Paul, would come into the business with him, but so far he hadn't had much luck in seducing Paul away from his own film career. At thirty-two, Paul was already a very successful young producer. He was far more successful at it than his father had been, and he genuinely loved it. But Jack had a profound distrust of the insecurities of the film industry, and its almost inevitable disappointments. And he would have given anything to lure Paul into the business. Maybe one day. But surely not for the moment. Paul didn't want to hear it.

Paul loved his work, and his wife. He had been married for the past two years, and the only thing that seemed to be missing from his life, or so he claimed, was a baby. Jack wasn't even sure how much Paul cared, but it was obvious that Jan did. She worked in an art gallery, and Jack always had the impression that she was just hanging around, waiting to have kids. She was a little bland for him, but she was a nice girl, and she obviously made Paul very happy. She was also beautiful; her mother was the long-retired but spectacular-looking actress Amanda Robbins. She was long, lean, and blonde, still wonderful to look at, at fifty. She had given up an extraordinary movie career twenty-six years before to marry a very staid, respectable, and as far as Jack was concerned, extremely boring banker named Matthew Kingston. They had two beautiful daughters, a huge house in Bel Air, and moved in the most respectable circles.

Amanda was one of the few women in Los Angeles who never shopped at Jack's store, and it always amused him, on the rare occasions when their paths crossed, to realize that she absolutely couldn't stand him. She seemed to hate everything he was, and everything he represented. And it wouldn't have surprised him at all to learn that Amanda had done everything in her power to dissuade her daughter from marrying Paul Watson. She and her husband seemed to take a dim view of show business, and they had been sure that eventually Paul would turn out to be just as promiscuous as his father. But he wasn't. Paul was a serious young man, and he had already proven to them that he was a solid, reliable husband. They had eventually accepted him into the fold of their family, although they had never warmed to his father. Jack's reputation was well known in L.A. He was good-looking, seen everywhere, and famous for cruising in and out of bed with every starlet and model who crossed his path, and he made no apology for it. He was always kind to the women he went out with, too much so, in fact. He was generous, intelligent, nice to be around, and always fun to be with. The women he went out with always adored him, and now and then one of them was even foolish enough to think they might "catch" him for more than just a brief affair. But Jack Watson was too smart for that. He saw to it that they came and went out of his life before they could settle down, or have time to start leaving their clothes in his closet. And he was always painfully honest with them, he made no promises, created no false impressions. He gave them a good time, took them to all the places they had ever read about or dreamed of, wined and dined them in the best restaurants, and before they knew what had hit them, he had moved on, to the next one. And they were left with a pleasant, albeit brief, memory of an affair with a handsome, sexy man, who left them gasping for more, and wishing they had been able to hang on to him for just a little longer.

It was impossible to be angry at Jack, or even stay that way for long. Everything about him was irresistibly charming, even the way he left them. He dated married women once in a while, but had only the nicest things to say about their husbands. Jack Watson was a fun guy, terrific in bed and an incurable playboy, and never pretended for a millisecond to be anything different. And at fifty-nine, he still looked a dozen years younger. He worked out when he had time, swam in the ocean frequently, still had his house in Malibu, and he loved his women nearly as much as his red Ferrari. The only things he really did care about, and was serious about, were his children. Julie and Paul were the lights of his life, and always would be. Their mother was only a dim memory, and one that still made him grateful whenever he thought of her, that she had had the good sense to leave him. For the past eighteen years, he had done exactly what he wanted, even when he was with Dori. He was spoiled, he had money, his business was a huge success, and he was irresistible to women, and what's more, he knew it. Though oddly, there was nothing arrogant about him. He was sexy, and fun, and almost always happy. He loved to have a good time. "Adorable" was a word women often used to describe him. They liked him, and he liked them.

" 'Morning, Jack." The manager of Julie's smiled at him, as he hurried through the store to the private elevator that would take him up to his office. It was on the fourth floor, and was entirely done in steel and black leather. It had been designed for him by a very famous Italian interior designer, yet another woman he had been involved with. She had wanted to leave her architect husband and three kids for him, and he had assured her that living with him would have driven her completely crazy. And by the time their affair ended, he had actually convinced her. Just watching Jack move around his own little world was both exciting and somewhat alarming.

He knew there would be coffee waiting for him

upstairs, and eventually a light lunch. He glanced at his watch. He was late for once. He had decided to be half an hour late for work in order to swim in the ocean, although it was January, but the weather had been warm, even if the water wasn't. He loved swimming in the ocean, loved his house at the beach, and everything about his business. And despite his playing the field with women, he was relentlessly disciplined about his work. It was no accident that Julie's was one of the most successful small chains in the retail business. Several people had approached him over the years about taking it public, but he still wasn't ready to do it. He liked maintaining control, and being the sole owner. He had no one else to consult about his decisions, no one to answer to, no one to badger him or explain to. Julie's was one hundred percent his baby.

When he got to his office, there was a stack of messages neatly laid out on his desk, a list of appointments he had that afternoon, and some swatches he had been expecting from Paris. They were nothing short of splendid. It was Dori who had introduced him to the miracle of French fabrics . . . and French food . . . and French wine . . . and French women. He still had a soft spot for them, and a lot of the merchandise he carried at Julie's were imports. The best of everything, that was what they promised, and delivered.

The phone rang almost as soon as he sat down, it

was the intercom, and he pressed the button as he continued to glance at the French fabrics.

"Hi." He spoke into the machine casually, in the voice that made women ache for him, but not his secretary, Gladdie. She knew him too well to be affected by him. She had worked for him for five years, and knew everything there was to know about him. And the one group of women who were sacred to him, that he never messed around with, were the ones who worked for him in his office. It was one of the few rules about women in his life that he had never broken. "Who is it?"

"Paul's on the line. Do you want to talk to him, or shall I tell him you're busy? Your ten-fifteen should be here any minute."

"He can wait." It was an appointment he had made to talk to a handbag manufacturer from Milan who dealt mostly in alligator and lizard. "You keep track of the guy for a few minutes when he gets here. I want to talk to Paul first." If possible, he tried not to put off his children, and he was smiling as he picked up the receiver. Paul was a great kid, he always had been, and Jack was crazy about him. "Hi there, what's doing?"

"I thought I'd call and see if you wanted me to pick you up, or if you'd rather meet us there." Although he was quiet by nature, unlike Jack, today he sounded unusually somber.

"Meet you where?" Paul's offer to pick him up touched no chord of memory. He had no recollection whatsoever of making an appointment with him and usually, when it concerned his children at least, he remembered, but not this time.

"Come on, Dad." Paul sounded mildly exasperated and somewhat stressed. He was clearly not amused by what his father was saying. "This is serious. Don't joke about it."

"I'm not joking," Jack said, setting the handful of French fabrics down, and glancing at the papers on his desk for some clue to what his son was saying. "Where are we going?" And then in a rush of embarrassment, he remembered. "Oh Christ, I . . ." Paul's father-in-law's funeral. How on earth could he have forgotten? But he hadn't written it down, and he must not have told Gladdie he was going, or she would have reminded him both the evening before and that morning.

"You forgot, didn't you, Dad?" Paul's voice was suddenly full of accusation. It was obvious that he didn't want to be messed around with. "I can't believe it."

"I didn't forget, I just wasn't thinking about it."

"Bullshit. You forgot. The service is at noon, there's a luncheon afterward at the house. You don't have to go to that, but I think it would be nice if you were there." His sister, Julie, had also promised to be there.

"How many people do you think they're having?" Jack asked, wondering suddenly how to rearrange several of his afternoon appointments. This wasn't going to be easy, but it meant something to Paul, so he would try to do it.

"At the lunch? I don't know . . . they know an awful lot of people, probably two or three hundred." Jack had been stunned to see more than five hundred people at his son's wedding. People had come from all over the country, mostly because of the Kingstons.

"Then they'll never miss me at the lunch," Jack said matter-of-factly, "and thanks for offering to pick me up. I'll meet you there. You should probably be with Jan and her mother and sister anyway. I'll stay somewhat in the distance."

"Make sure Amanda knows you were there," Paul instructed. "Jan would be very upset if her mom thought you hadn't come to the funeral."

"She'd probably be a lot happier if I didn't," Jack laughed, making no bones about the mild animosity between them. He had danced with her a couple of times at the wedding, and Amanda Kingston made it clear without saying a word that she thoroughly disliked him. Like everyone else in town, she read about him constantly in the papers. And since giving up her career, she had adopted her husband's very sober view that one should only be in the newspapers when one was born, died, or got married. Jack was usually in the papers for being seen with some moderately well-known actress, or budding starlet, or for giving a bash of some kind at Julie's. The store was famous, as was he, for its fabulous parties for their designers and clients. People begged for invitations to them, but certainly not the Kingstons. And knowing they wouldn't come, he had never bothered to invite them.

"Anyway, be on time, Dad. You'd be late to your own funeral, if you could."

"Which, hopefully, won't be for a while, thank you very much," Jack said, thinking of the heart attack that had killed Matthew Kingston. He had died four days before, on the tennis court, and he was two years younger than Jack. Amanda had just turned fifty. The men who had been playing tennis with him had done everything possible to revive him, but they had been unable to do it. At fifty-seven, he was being mourned by his family, the entire banking community, and all those who knew him. But Jack had never liked him. He thought he was pompous, stuffy, and boring.

"I'll see you there, Dad. I have to pick up Jan at her mom's. She spent the night there."

"Does she need anything? A hat? A dress? I can have one of the girls pull some things for you to pick up on your way over there if you need it."

"That's okay, Dad." Paul smiled at his father's voice. He was a pain in the ass sometimes, but he was basically a decent guy, and Paul loved him. "I think Amanda got them everything they needed. She's in pretty bad shape over Matt, but she's incredibly organized, even now. She's an amazing woman."

"The Ice Queen," Jack said, and then regretted it

instantly, but the words slipped out before he could stop them.

"That's a lousy thing to say about a woman who just lost her husband."

"Sorry. I wasn't thinking." But he wasn't far off the mark. She always looked and seemed totally in control, and absolutely perfect. Just looking at her always gave Jack an almost irresistible urge to mess her up and take her clothes off. The very thought of it even now somehow struck him funny as he hung up the phone, and thought about her, which was something he did very seldom.

He was sorry about her loss, and he still remembered all too well how he had felt when Dori had died, but there was something so distant and cold about Paul's mother-in-law that it made it hard to really empathize much with her. She was so goddamn unbearably perfect. And she still looked incredibly like the way she had when she was Amanda Robbins, and left the screen at twenty-four to marry Matthew Kingston. It had been a huge Hollywood and society wedding, and for years people had guessed and made bets about whether or not she'd get bored and come back into the business. But she didn't. She kept her looks, and her icy beauty, but her career was over forever. It was also easy to believe that Matthew Kingston would never have let her. He acted as though he owned her.

Jack opened the closet in his dressing room, and was glad to see he had left a dark suit in it. It wasn't one of his best, but at least it was appropriate for the occasion, although all the ties he found in the small collection he kept there for emergencies were either red, bright blue, or yellow. He quickly strode out to his outer office to find Gladdie.

"Why didn't you remind me about the funeral?" He scowled at her, but he wasn't really angry and she knew it. He was one of those rare people who always took responsibility for his own mistakes, which was one of the many reasons why she loved working for him. And despite his reputation for being flip and irresponsible, she actually knew him a great deal better. As an employer, he was caring, generous, reliable, and a real pleasure to work for.

"I just thought you had it worked out. Did you forget?" she asked with a smile, and with a sheepish grin, he nodded.

"Freudian, I guess. I hate going to the funerals of men who are younger than I am. Do me a favor, Glad, run down the street to Hermès and get me a dark tie. Nothing too miserable, but just serious enough so I don't embarrass Paul. Nothing with naked women on it." She laughed at him, and grabbed her purse just as the handbag manufacturer and his assistant came in. It was going to be a very quick meeting.

Jack had ordered a hundred bags by eleven o'clock, and Gladdie was back from Hermès by then with a slate-gray tie with tiny little white geometric figures on it. It was perfect. "You do good work," he said gratefully, as he put it around his neck and tied it impeccably without looking in the mirror. He was wearing a dark gray suit and a white shirt, and hand-made French oxfords. And he looked incredibly handsome with sandy blond hair, warm brown eyes, and chiseled features. "Do I look respectable?"

"I'm not sure that's a word I'd use for you . . . maybe beautiful is more like it." She smiled at him, totally inured to his charms, which he always found very pleasing about her. Being with Gladdie was al-ways very soothing. She didn't give a damn about his looks or his reputation, or his womanizing, just about his business. "You look great, honest. Paul will be proud of you."

"I hope so. Maybe his charming mother-in-law will even refrain from calling the vice squad when she sees me coming. God, I hate funerals." He could already feel a pall falling over him, it still reminded him of Dori. Christ, that had been awful . . . the shock, and the unbearable pain of it. The sheer mis-ery of trying to understand that she was gone for-ever. It had taken him years to get over it, although he had tried to fill the void with a thousand women. But there had never been another woman like her. She was so warm, so beautiful, so sexy and mischie-vous and appealing. She was sensational, and just thinking about her, as he rode the elevator down-stairs in his somber outfit shortly before noon, genu-inely depressed him. It had been twelve years since she died, and he still missed her.

Jack didn't even notice the women watching him
admiringly as he left the store, and slid behind the
wheel of his Ferrari. He peeled it away from the curb
with immediate speed, and a roar of the powerful
engine, and five minutes later he was on Santa
Monica Boulevard, heading toward All Saints Episcopal Church, where they were holding the service.
It was ten after noon by then, and traffic was worse
than he had expected. It was a warm January afternoon in L.A., and everyone in the world seemed to
be in their car and going somewhere. He was twenty
minutes late when he got to All Saints and slipped
quietly into a pew at the back of the church. He
couldn't even imagine how many people were there.
From where he was sitting it looked like seven or
eight hundred, but he was sure it couldn't be that
many.

He tried to catch a glimpse of his daughter, Julie,
but she was lost in the crowd somewhere. And he
couldn't even see Paul at the front of the church,
sitting between his wife and her sister. And his view
of the widow was completely obscured. All Jack
could see and think about was the inexorable inevita-
bility of the coffin, so stark and severe, a rich mahog-
any with brass handles, covered by a carpet of moss
and tiny white orchids. It was beautiful in its own
grim way, as were the rest of the flowers in the
church. There were orchids everywhere, and somehow without thinking about it, Jack knew that
Amanda had done it. There was the same kind of

impeccable attention to detail, even at a time like this, that she had shown during their children's wedding.

But Jack quickly forgot about her, and sat lost in his own thoughts, reminded of his own mortality, during the High Episcopal service. A friend spoke, and both sons-in-law. Paul's words were brief and to the point, but very moving, and in spite of himself there were tears in Jack's eyes when he praised his son for it after the service.

"That was very nice, Son," he said, sounding hoarse for a moment. "You can speak at mine, when the time comes." He tried to make light of it, but Paul shook his head with a look of disgust and put an arm around his father's shoulders.

"Don't flatter yourself. I couldn't say a single decent thing about you, and neither could anyone else, so don't bother."

"Thanks, I'll keep it in mind. Maybe I should give up tennis."

"Dad . . ." Paul scolded, with a quick warning look. Amanda was approaching, moving quietly through the crowd to the place where she would stand to greet a few of the mourners. And before Jack could move, he found he was looking right at her. She looked amazingly beautiful, and in spite of the years since, still very much a movie star. She was wearing a huge black hat and veil, and a very distinguished black suit, which he suspected immediately had probably been made by a French designer.

"Hello, Jack," she said calmly. She seemed very much in control, yet the huge blue eyes held so much pain, that he actually felt sorry for her.

"I'm sorry, Amanda." Even if he wasn't fond of her, it was easy to see how ravaged she was by the loss of her husband. There wasn't much else he could say to her, as she looked away and bowed her head for a moment, and then an instant later she moved on, and Paul went to find Jan, who was standing with her sister.

Jack stayed for another minute or two, saw no one he knew, and then decided to leave quietly without bothering his son. Paul obviously had his hands full.

And half an hour later, Jack was back in his office, but he was quiet all afternoon, thinking about them, the family that had lost the man who held them all together. Even if he hadn't liked him, one had to respect him, and feel sorry for the loved ones he had left so swiftly. And all afternoon, no matter what he did, Jack was haunted by Dori. He even took out a photograph of her, something he rarely did, but he kept one way at the back of his desk, for just such moments. And looking down at her smiling face on the beach at Saint-Tropez made him feel more bereft than ever.

Gladdie checked on him once or twice, and sensed that he wanted to be left alone. He even had her cancel his last two appointments. But even depressed, he looked great in the dark suit and the tie she had bought him. And he had no idea that, at that exact moment, in the house in Bel Air, Amanda Kingston was talking about him.

"It was nice of your father to come," she said to Paul, as the last of their guests finally left them. It had been an endless afternoon for all of them, and despite her unshakable poise, even Amanda looked exhausted.

"He felt very badly about Matthew," Paul said, touching her arm sympathetically, as she nodded and looked at her daughters.

Both girls were devastated by the loss of their father, and for once, they had even stopped fighting. Jan and her sister, Louise, were only slightly more than a year apart, but in every possible way they were entirely different. And they had battled with each other, night and day, ever since their childhood. But, at least for now, they had made peace in order to comfort their mother. And Paul left them alone quietly, as he went out to the kitchen to help himself to a cup of coffee. The catering staff was still there, clearing away the dishes and glasses left behind by more than three hundred people who had come to pay their respects to the Kingstons.

"I can't believe he's gone," Amanda said in a whisper, standing with her back to both girls, looking out over their perfectly manicured garden.

"Neither can I," Jan said, as tears rolled down her cheeks again, and Louise sighed audibly. She had loved him, but she had never gotten along with her father. She always thought he'd been harder on her than he was on Jan, and expected more of her. He had been furious with her when she had decided not to go to law school and had gotten married right out of college. But the marriage was a solid one, and in the first five years she had borne three children. But he had even had something to say about that. He thought she was having too many children. It didn't bother him at all that Jan had never had a real career, nor even wanted one, and had married a man who worked in show business and had a father who was nothing more than a Rodeo Drive merchant. Louise didn't like Paul, and made no bones about it. Her own husband was a Loeb and Loeb attorney and more suitable for a Kingston to marry.

But as Jan cried on the afternoon of the funeral, all Louise could think of was how much her father had criticized her, how difficult he had been, and how often she had wondered if he even loved her. She would have liked to say something about it, but she knew that neither her mother nor sister would understand. Her mother always hated it when she said anything critical about her father. And as far as her mother was concerned, he was already a saint now.

"I want you both to remember how wonderful he was," Amanda said as she turned back to them, her chin quivering and her eyes filled with tears. She wore her blond hair straight back in a bun, and as they were both acutely aware, she was far more beautiful than they were, and always had been. She was an extraordinary beauty, and Louise always hated that about her. Her mother was almost impossible to live up to, and she had always expected both of them to be so perfect. Louise had never really understood the more human side of her, the vulnerability, the insecurities that had followed her throughout her life and lurked behind the exquisite facade. It was Jan who was much closer to their mother, which spawned the continuing resentment between both sisters. Louise had always accused Jan of being their parents' favorite, and Jan had always felt unfairly accused and couldn't see it.

"I want you both to know how very, very much he loved you," Amanda continued, and then couldn't go on as she began to sob softly. She couldn't believe he was gone, couldn't believe he would never hold her in his arms again. It was her worst nightmare come true. He had been everything she depended on, and she couldn't even begin to imagine a life without him.

"Oh, Mom." Jan cradled her mother in her arms like a child as her mother sobbed, and Louise quietly left the room and found Paul in the kitchen. He was sitting at the kitchen table, drinking a cup of coffee.

"How is she?" he asked, looking concerned, and Louise shrugged, her own pain visible, but, as usual, mixed with anger. Her kids had gone home with the baby-sitter, and her husband had gone back to the office. And there was no one else but Paul to talk to, whether or not she liked him.

"She's a mess. She was completely dependent on him. He told her when to get up and when to go to bed, what to do, and not do, and who she could be friends with. I don't know why she let him do that to her. It was disgusting."

"Maybe that was what she needed," Paul said, looking at his wife's sister with interest. She was always so filled with anger and resentment, and he secretly wondered how happy she really was with her husband. Like all families, they all had their secret agendas and hidden undercurrents. And it always intrigued him to hear the girls talk about their mother. They each saw her differently, but the woman they knew was so different from the cool facade she presented to the world. They saw someone completely dominated and privately frightened. He wondered if that was the real reason why she had never gone back to making movies. Maybe aside from Matthew not wanting her to, she was just too afraid to do it. "She'll be all right," he reassured Louise, not knowing what else to say to her, as she poured a glass of wine for herself. She showed too many of the signs of an unhappy woman.

"Jan'll keep an eye on her," he said to soothe his sister-in-law, but the remark only enraged her.

"Yeah, I'll bet she will. She's always sucking up to her. She always did, even when we were kids. I'm surprised the two of you don't offer to move in with her, that might really impress her. You know, she'll need a lot of help with settling the estate. I'm sure

you and Jan will be only too happy to help her do it."

"Why don't you relax, Lou?" he said, using Jan's name for her, and she glanced at him with smoldering eyes that were surprisingly like her mother's. But other than that, she looked just like her father, handsome, but no more than that. Between the two, Jan was the better looking. "No one's trying to hurt you."

"Too late for that," she said, pouring another glass of wine as soon as she finished the first one. "They've been doing it for years. Maybe Mom'll grow up now, without Daddy. Maybe we all will," she said, set down the glass and walked out into the garden, and Paul made no move to follow.

And from inside the study where they sat, Jan and Amanda saw her through the window. "She's mad at me again," Jan said. "She's always mad at me about something."

"I wish you two would stop fighting," Amanda said sadly, looking at her younger daughter. "I always thought when you grew up it would be different, that you'd be the best of friends, especially once you were both married and had children." It was all she had ever envisioned for them since they were babies, but there was a look of sorrow in Jan's eyes almost as soon as her mother said it.

"Well, I don't . . . do I. . . ."

"What?" Her mother looked confused for a moment, and so sad it broke Jan's heart to see her.

"Have children." Something about the way she said it caught her mother's attention.

"Don't you want to have children?" Amanda looked shocked, as though the very idea that her daughter didn't want children would be a betrayal.

"Yes," Jan nodded, and looked at her sister through the window. Lou had had three kids in five years, as easy as pie, as soon as she wanted. And this time it was Jan who was jealous of her. "Of course I do. We've been trying for a year, and nothing has happened."

"That doesn't mean anything," Amanda smiled at her. "Sometimes it takes a while. Just be patient."

"It didn't take you 'a while.' You and Daddy had us in the first two years you were married." She sighed then, as Amanda patted her hand, and then she looked up at her mother. And what Amanda saw in her eyes tore her heart out, it was not only grief, but fear and bitter disappointment. "I want Paul to go to a doctor with me, but he won't do it. He thinks I'm crazy to be worried."

"Did you talk to the doctor yourself, does he think there's a problem?" Amanda was beginning to look seriously concerned about her.

"He doesn't know, but he thinks it's worth looking into. He gave me the name of a specialist, but Paul was furious when I told him. He said his sister has kids, and so does Lou. There's no reason why we should have a problem. But it's not always that simple." Amanda wondered suddenly if there was some-

thing she didn't know, a terrible disease in her daughter's youth, an indiscretion, an abortion, but she didn't dare ask her. It was better to leave that to her doctor.

"Well then, maybe you should listen to Paul, at least for a while, and try not to worry about it."

"It's all I think of, Mom," she confessed, as tears ran down her cheeks and spilled onto her dress as her mother watched her in anguish. "I want a baby so much . . . and I'm so scared I'll never have one."

"Of course you will . . ." She couldn't bear the thought of seeing her daughter so unhappy, especially now, with having just lost her father. "You can always adopt, if it doesn't happen later."

"Paul says he'll never do that. He wants his *own* children." Amanda had to hold her tongue, so as not to tell her that Paul sounded not only difficult, but extremely opinionated and selfish.

"You can cross that bridge later. For right now, why don't you just try to relax, and I'll bet you anything, it'll happen before you know it." Jan nodded, but it was obvious from the look in her eyes that she was anything but convinced now. She had been worrying about it for an entire year, and concern was rapidly turning to panic. But if nothing else, a door had opened between mother and daughter.

"What about you, Mom? Are you going to be okay without Dad?" It was an agonizing question, and brought tears to Amanda's eyes again as she shook her head and wept.

"I can't even imagine living without him. There will never be anyone else in my life, Jan. Never. I couldn't bear it. We've been married for twenty-six years, more than half my lifetime. I can't even begin to think about what I'll do now . . . how do I wake up every morning. . . ." Jan took her mother in her arms and let her cry, wishing she could promise her that she'd feel better, but she couldn't imagine her mother living without him either. He had been the life force of their family, he had shielded Amanda from the world, told her what to do about everything, and although he was only seven years older than she, in some ways he had been like a father to her. "I just can't live without him," she said, and Jan knew she meant it. They sat and talked about him for another hour, and then finally Paul came back into the room. Lou had left without saying good-bye, she had been crying when she left, after watching them through the window, and Paul had work to do at home. It was nearly six o'clock by then, and sooner or later, they had to leave Amanda, no matter how hard it was for her. She had to learn to face life alone.

She looked so pathetic as they left, standing on the front steps of the Bel Air house in her black suit, waving at them, that Jan burst into tears again the moment they turned the corner.

"My God, Paul, she's just going to die without Daddy." She couldn't stop crying at the thought of the father she had lost, the sister who hated her, the mother who was in so much pain, and the baby she feared would never come her way. It was all completely overwhelming, and Paul held her hand as they drove home and tried to reassure her.

"She'll be fine in a while. You'll see. Just look at her, she's still young and beautiful. Hell, in six months, she'll have all of Los Angeles pounding on her door, asking her out. Maybe she'll even go back to the movies. She's certainly young enough to do it."

"She'd never do that, even if she wanted to, because she knows that Daddy never wanted her to go back to making movies. He wanted her to himself, and she did it because she loved him." Paul didn't say that if that was true Matthew Kingston was probably the most selfish man who had ever lived, because he knew Jan would have killed him if he said it. "And how could you suggest my mother would go out with anyone? That's disgusting."

"It's not disgusting," he said quietly. "It's real. She's fifty years old, Jan. And your father died, she didn't. You can't really expect her to stay alone forever." He said it with a small smile, and Jan looked furious as she glanced at him.

"Of course she's not going to go out with anyone. She's not your father, for God's sake. She had a wonderful marriage, and she loved Daddy."

"Then she'll probably want to get married again. It would be a crime if she didn't."

"I can't believe what you just said," Jan said breathlessly, pulling her hand away from his, and staring at him. "You actually think my mother is going to go out with *men?* You're sick, and you have no respect for anything. And furthermore, you don't know my mother."

"I guess not, sweetheart," he said soothingly. "But I do know people." She said not another word to him, and stared out the window away from him, furious at what he'd said, as they drove home in silence. Jan would have willingly sworn on a stack of Bibles that her mother would be faithful to her husband's memory for the rest of her life.

Chapter Two

Amanda Kingston took both her daughters to the Biltmore in Santa Barbara in June. Paul was in New York, working on the last details of a movie deal, and Louise's husband, Jerry, was at a legal conference in Denver. And it seemed an ideal opportunity to spend some time together. But as soon as they got to the hotel, and actually sat down and talked, both younger women realized how badly their mother was doing. She still wore black constantly, her hair was pulled tightly back and looked too severe, and she wore no makeup, and as soon as Jan asked how she was, she burst into tears and couldn't stop crying.

It was one of those rare times when both girls put down their animosity, and were united in concern for their mother. And while Amanda was still asleep, they both went downstairs to the dining room for breakfast together on Sunday morning.

"She should see a doctor. She's just too depressed," Louise said over blueberry pancakes. "She scares me. I think she ought to be on Prozac . . . or Valium, or something."

"That'll just make her worse. She needs to get out and see her friends. I ran into Mrs. Auberman last week and she said she hasn't seen Mom since Dad died. It's been five months, she can't just sit in the house and cry forever."

"Maybe she can," Louise said, looking her sister in the eye, wondering, as she always did, if they had anything at all in common. "You know, it's what Dad would have wanted. If he could have left instructions to that effect, he would have had her buried with him."

"That's *disgusting.*" Jan looked at her older sister with instant fury. "You know how he hated it when she was unhappy!"

"You know how he hated it when she had any kind of a life other than watching us take ballet, or playing bridge with the wives of his partners. I think that subconsciously she thinks he would have wanted her to be just as miserable as she is. I think she should see a shrink," Louise said bluntly.

"Why don't we take her on a vacation?" It seemed like a nice idea to Jan, who had an easy time taking time off from the gallery, but Louise didn't see how she could leave her children. "Maybe in September, when they're back in school. We could take her to Paris."

"Sounds good to me," Louise said, but when they suggested it to Amanda at lunch, she immediately shook her head, and said she couldn't.

"I couldn't possibly get away now," she said firmly, "I still have too much to do for the estate. I don't want that hanging over my head forever." But they all knew it was an excuse. She just didn't want to rejoin the world of the living, not without Matthew.

"Let the lawyers take care of it, Mom," Lou said practically, "they do anyway. It would do you good to get away."

She hesitated for a long moment, and then shook her head as tears filled her eyes again, and she was honest with them. "I don't want to. I'd feel too guilty."

"For what? Spending a little money? You can certainly afford a trip to Paris." Or many, many of them, as they all knew. That was not the issue. But the real problem was far deeper.

"It's not that, I just . . . I just feel that I don't have the right to do something like that without Matthew. . . . Why should I go out and kick up my heels? Why should I have a good time?" She began to sob, but she had to say it, as both girls watched her. "Why am I still alive and he isn't? It's so unfair. Why did it have to happen?" She had survivor guilt, and neither of them had ever heard her say it.

"It just happened, Mom," Jan said gently. "It just did. It wasn't your fault, or his, or anyone's. It was just horrible rotten luck, but you have to go on living . . . for yourself . . . for us . . . just think about it. If you don't want to go to Paris, we'll go to New York for a few days, or San Francisco. But you have to do something. You can't just give up on life, Mom. Daddy wouldn't have wanted you to do that." But it was obvious, just talking to her on the drive home, that she wasn't ready to do it. She was still too deep in mourning for her husband to even want to go on living, or think about doing anything constructive or amusing.

"How's she doing?" Paul asked when he flew back from New York on Sunday night, and Jan drove him home from the airport.

"She isn't. She's a total mess. Lou thinks she should be on Prozac. I don't know what I think. It's as if she's tried to bury herself with Daddy."

"Maybe that was what he would have wanted. Maybe she knows that."

"You sound just like my sister," Jan said, looking out the window, and then back at him. "I want to ask you something." She said it so solemnly that he smiled at her. He was happy to see her after the trip to New York. He had really missed her.

"Sure. You want me to fix her up with my father? No problem. I'll arrange it. He'd love it." The idea was so outrageous that even Jan laughed, but an instant later, her eyes were serious again, and whatever it was, he could sense that it was important to her.

"I have something else in mind," she said nervously, not sure how to broach it to him, but desperate to convince him.

"Spit it out, Jan. I'm waiting."

"I want both of us to go to the doctor. The specialist. It's been six months since the last time we talked about it, and nothing has happened." She looked earnest and terrified as she asked, but Paul looked less than sympathetic.

"Christ, that again. You never let up, do you? I've been working on the biggest film deal of my career for the past six months, and all you can think about is a baby. No wonder it hasn't happened, Jan. I've been on airplanes more than I've been home. How can you say we have a problem?" To her, it sounded like denial. There were always excuses, plausible things to blame it on, but the bottom line was she hadn't gotten pregnant and they had tried more than he was admitting.

"I just want to know if something is wrong. Maybe we're both fine, or maybe it's me. I want to know so we can deal with it. That's all, is that so much to ask?" Her eyes filled with tears as she said it, and he sighed, looking at her.

"Why don't you have him check you out? And by the time he does, you'll probably be pregnant." But she no longer thought so, it had been just over a year and a half since they started trying, and even her gynecologist was concerned now, and had urged her to explore it further, if she was serious about having a baby. She didn't tell Paul she had been to see the specialist alone three weeks before, and so far he had found nothing wrong with her, which meant that Paul had to go now.

"Will you go too, after I do?"

"Maybe" was all he would commit to, and with that, he turned the radio on a little too loud, and Jan stared sadly out the window. It was beginning to seem hopeless to her, especially given Paul's attitude.

By August, the specialist had confirmed to her that there was nothing wrong with her, and that either his sperm and her eggs were incompatible in some way, or perhaps the problem, if there was one, was her husband's. But when she brought it up again, Paul was furious with her, he didn't want to be pressured. It was a bad time for him, his big deal was falling through, and he was sick to death of having sex on schedule, and then having her get hysterical two weeks later when she found she wasn't pregnant.

"Just forget it for a while!" he shouted at her one night when she wanted him to make love to her because the time was right. And then he went out for a drink with his father. Jack was seeing someone new, an actress everyone had heard of, and he was in the papers again, almost daily. He also wanted more than ever for Paul to come into the business with him, which as far as Paul was concerned was out of the question. He felt as though everyone in his life wanted something from him.

And in September, Louise and Jan tried to talk Amanda into a trip again, but got nowhere. She had lost fourteen pounds, and looked too thin, and she was still depressed and going nowhere. And by December, both daughters were panicked.

"We've got to do something," Jan said frantically on the phone to Louise one afternoon, two weeks after Thanksgiving, which had been ghastly. Their mother had cried all through the meal, and she was in such dismal shape, she had even upset the children. "I can't stand it anymore."

"Maybe we should just leave her alone," Louise said philosophically. "Maybe this is how she wants to spend the rest of her life without Daddy. Who are we to decide it should be different?"

"We're her children, and we can't just let her live like this. I won't let her."

"Then you figure out something. She doesn't want to hear it from me. She never does. You're the favorite. You go to her house every day and slip pills into her orange juice. I think she has a right to live any way she wants to."

"Louise, she's dying, for chrissake," Jan said miserably. "Can't you see what's happening to her? She has completely given up on life. She might as well have died with Daddy."

"I don't have the answers, Jan. She's a grown woman, and I'm not a psychiatrist. And frankly, I'm sick to death of watching her feel sorry for herself. I hate seeing her, I hate listening to her. It's pathetic, but she loves it. She's wallowing in guilt because she's alive, and Daddy isn't. So let her. Maybe in some sick way she's happy."

"I won't let her do it," Jan insisted.

"You can't bring her to life again, Jan. She has to *want* to do it, and she doesn't. Face it. For once in her life, she's in control of her own life, and maybe this is how she wants to live it. At least Daddy's not telling her what to do now."

"You make him sound like a monster," Jan complained.

"He was sometimes. To me anyway."

As usual, the sisters couldn't agree on anything.

And the week before Christmas, Paul and Jan got an invitation from Paul's father to come to a Christmas bash at Julie's. Jan wasn't in the mood for it this year. Paul was still refusing to see the specialist, and Jan was depressed about it, and worried about her mother. But Paul said his father's feelings would be hurt if they didn't make an effort to at least drop in at the party.

"Why don't you go without me?" Jan said to Paul when the morning of the party came. She just didn't feel like going. "I promised my mother I'd come by to see her this afternoon, and I'll probably feel even worse once I see her." She was sliding steadily downhill from life to death, and watching her do it was driving Jan crazy. She felt entirely helpless to stop her.

"Why don't you bring your mother with you?" he suggested offhandedly as he left for work, and Jan looked at him with total irritation.

"Haven't you listened to anything I've said to you for the past year? She's depressed, she's losing weight, she's not seeing anyone. She's just sitting there waiting to die, for chrissake. Do you really think she'd come to one of your father's jazzy parties? You're dreaming."

"Maybe it would do her good. Ask her at least." He said it with a smile, and Jan wanted to throw something at him. He just didn't get it.

"You don't know my mother."

"Just ask her."

"I might as well ask her to take all her clothes off and run naked through the streets of Bel Air, for chrissake."

"At least the neighbors would be happy." Even depressed, she was still a spectacular-looking woman. He had even had a crazy idea about asking her to be in his next movie, but he was afraid to ask Jan what she thought about it. He already knew what she'd tell him. "Anyway, tell her my father would be thrilled if she'd come. It would lend the store respectability," he teased, as he kissed her good-bye, and in spite of herself, she let him. She was deeply upset with him for still not seeing the doctor about their inability to have a baby, and she was beginning to think, and had for a while, that there would never be children in their future. In some ways, she was almost as depressed as her mother, she just didn't show it, but most days she felt as bad as her mother.

But when she saw Amanda that afternoon, it broke Jan's heart to see her. She looked thin and tired and pale and as though she had nothing left to live for. At fifty, Amanda felt as though her life were over. Jan tried everything, suggested everything she could think of, she cajoled, she begged, she threatened, she told her that if she didn't pull herself together soon, she and Louise would come and stay with her and drag her out of the house if they had to.

"You girls have better things to do with your time than worry about me. How is Paul's new movie?" She always changed the subject, and the focus of the conversation, to something else, but by the end of the afternoon, Jan was so upset she was actually angry with her, and she said so.

"You know, you make me mad as hell. You have everything to be grateful for, a good life, a beautiful home, two daughters who love you, and all you can do is sit here and feel sorry for yourself and cry over Daddy. Don't you even love us, Mom? Can't you think of anyone but yourself for once? Don't you see how worried we are? Christ, that's all I ever think about anymore. That and the fact that I'm never going to have children." And without meaning to, she was suddenly crying and her mother had her arms around her, and was holding her, and apologizing for the pain and concern she'd caused them. They were both crying, but for once, the things Jan had said were cathartic, and her mother actually looked a little better. "You don't even wear makeup anymore, Mom. You don't dress. Your hair looks awful." It felt good to be honest with her, and for once Amanda laughed through her tears and looked in the mirror appraisingly. And what she saw there was not pleasant. What they both saw in the mirror was a beautiful woman, sad and pale and neglected. And suddenly Jan decided to try Paul's tactic. She told her mother about Jack's party that night at Julie's.

"Go *there?* To the *store?*" As Jan had predicted she would, Amanda looked horrified at the suggestion. "That's crazy."

"So is what you've done to yourself in the past year. Come on, Mommy, do it for me. You won't know anyone. Just put on a dress and some makeup and we'll go together. It would make Paul really happy."

"I'll go out to dinner with you both one night. He'd like that. I'll take you to Spago's."

"I want you to come out with me now. You don't have to stay long. Five minutes. Just make the effort. For me . . . for Lou . . . for Daddy . . . he wouldn't want to see you like this, Mom. I really believe that." She nearly held her breath as she looked at her mother. She was absolutely certain that there was no way her mother would go with her, but

Amanda stood very still, watching her for a long moment, uncertain.

"Do you really think your father would want me to do it?" she asked, as Jan nodded slowly. It was amazing how much that still meant to her.

"I do, Mom." It was a lie, but she wanted her mother to believe it, and then, nodding slowly, Amanda turned on her heel and walked into her bedroom, as Jan followed, in amazement. She didn't dare ask her mother what she was doing. But Amanda had marched into her closet, and Jan could hear rustling and the shifting of dresses. It was a full five minutes before she emerged again, carrying a somber black one.

"What do you think of this?" she asked, as Jan looked at her wide-eyed, unable to believe she'd done it. She had finally gotten through to her, and had somehow managed to dynamite her out of her house and her husband's grave. It was beyond amazing.

"I think it's a little severe, don't you?" She followed her mother back inside, afraid to discourage her completely, but the dress was really depressing. "How about this one?" She pointed to a purple one she knew her mother loved, but her father had loved it too, and Amanda shook her head the moment Jan showed it to her. Instead she chose a pretty navy blue wool dress that had always been too tight and now molded her figure beautifully, and was much younger-looking than the first one. It was, in its own way, as distinguished as she was, and she looked like the star she had once been as she tried it on in front of the mirror. She put on a pair of navy blue high-heel pumps, and a pair of sapphire earrings, and combed her hair back in the smooth knot that had been her signature in many of her pictures, and she put so little makeup on Jan couldn't even see it. "Maybe a little more, Mom? What do you think?" Amanda looked at herself appraisingly, into it now, and conceded.

"Maybe just a little. I don't want to look like a hooker."

"I think that would take some real work actually, more than we have time for." Jan smiled in pleasure as she looked at her mother. She looked spectacular, and like the woman she had known and loved all her life, not the scarecrow she had become in the past year, as she mourned her husband.

"What do you think?" Amanda asked nervously. "Do I look like me, or the sad sack I've been?" There were tears glistening in her eyes as she said it.

"You look like you, Mom," Jan said with tears in her own eyes, grateful to whatever Fates had finally convinced her mother. "Oh God, I love you," she said, as she held her. Amanda blew her nose daintily in a handkerchief, touched up her lipstick again with a practiced hand, and then put the few things she needed into a navy handbag, and looked admiringly at her daughter. Jan was wearing a red wool dress she loved and wore every Christmas, and standing side by side in red and blue, they looked almost like sisters.

"You're a good girl, Jan, and I love you," she whispered, as they headed toward the front door. Amanda still couldn't believe she'd let Jan talk her into this, but she was determined now to do it. "We won't stay long though, will we?" she asked nervously as she grabbed a mink coat from the closet in the front hall. She hadn't worn it since her husband's funeral, but she didn't let herself think of that now. She was doing this for her daughter. "I don't want to stay more than a few minutes."

"I'll bring you home whenever you want, Mom. I promise."

"All right then," she said, looking surprisingly young and vulnerable as she followed Jan through the front door, and as though to say good-bye to someone who wasn't there, she glanced over her shoulder for just an instant, paused, and then closed the door softly behind her.

Chapter Three

The preparations for the party at the store had gone on since early that morning. There were garlands over the doors, and wreaths in all the windows. They closed at four o'clock exactly, and there was a beautiful Christmas tree, all decorated in silver. Jack was pleased when he saw it.

"I know they're not politically correct anymore. But I love 'em. This one's a beauty." The store was sparkling as he looked around. There were bars in three locations, and cases of French Champagne chilling in the kitchen. And he had hired four musicians to play music, to liven up the atmosphere, but not for dancing. They were expecting two hundred people. It was one of their more exclusive parties, for only their best customers, and a list of celebrities that Jack knew would be there. Unlike their not showing up at most events, they always came to Jack's parties. Everybody loved him, and coming to parties at Julie's.

"Well, Gladdie, how does it look to you?" he asked, as he looked around for one last time before going to change. He had bought a new Armani suit for the occasion.

"Looks good to me, Jack. Really good," she said, as she admired all the details. She loved his parties. They were always terrific.

"Keep an eye on things for me. I'm going to go upstairs and change," he said, and disappeared into the elevator. He was back, looking like the cover on *GQ* twenty minutes later. The suit was dark blue, but there was nothing stuffy about it, and the way he wore it made him look like a male model.

"Very handsome," Gladdie said in an undertone when he came back downstairs again. "You look terrific. Do you have a date tonight?" she inquired with interest. The last starlet had passed through his hands several weeks before, and she knew he was currently cultivating a well-known model.

"At least a dozen of them," he laughed. "Unfortunately, Starr left for Paris this morning. But she had me invite her sister."

"Very generous of her . . . or very foolish . . ." Gladdie commented with a grin.

"I think she has a friend in Paris." He smiled,

feeling pleased with life, and pleasantly unencumbered, which was how he liked things.

"Are the kids coming tonight?" Gladdie asked, helping herself to a glass of Champagne as the first guests started to come through the door. Elizabeth Taylor had just walked in with Michael Jackson. And Barbra Streisand and a friend were right behind them.

"They said they'd try," Jack said absently as he went to greet his guests, and within half an hour the place was jumping. The music added to the festive mood, and celebrities came and went, as outside, photographers snapped their pictures, but Jack wouldn't allow them in the building. He wanted everyone to relax and enjoy the party, without fear of the press or the tabloids or the cameras.

It was nearly seven o'clock when Jan and Amanda drove up to the door, and Jan relinquished her car to the valet, and preceded her mother into Julie's. She had been worried on the way that Amanda would suddenly panic and change her mind, and the photographers who leapt at them instantly almost did it. But Jan pulled her into the store as quickly as she could, and Amanda looked suddenly breathless and a little startled when she got there. It was all so dazzling and so festive and so busy. There were faces she recognized everywhere, and two of the actresses she had worked with years before suddenly rushed up to her and threw their arms around her. They were obviously thrilled to see her and wanted to know everything she'd been doing. She managed to tell them about Matt, and that this was the first time she'd been out since he died. And from a little distance, Jan watched her proudly, as she walked over to say hello to her sister-in-law, Julie.

And from across the room, where he was talking to an old friend, Jack suddenly looked at them in amazement. "I don't believe it, . . ." he muttered under his breath and excused himself to greet Jan. "Would it be rude to say I'm stunned?" he whispered to her, glancing at Amanda, and Jan laughed as she whispered back to him.

"Not as stunned as I am. I've been trying to get her out of the house all year. This is the first time she's been out since Dad died, and probably the first time she's been to a party like this since she retired from the movies."

"I'm honored," he said, and sounded as though he meant it, and he waited patiently nearby for Amanda to finish her conversations, and then he walked up to her and thanked her for coming. "Julie's will never be the same again after this," he smiled at her. "You've finally given us the distinction I've always thought we deserved, but couldn't pull off without you." He was teasing her, but only a little.

"I doubt that, Jack. It's good to see you. It's a beautiful party. I've already run into lots of old friends here."

"I'm sure they're happy to see you. You'll have to come back more often. We'll throw a party for you anytime you want to come shopping." He seemed in good spirits, and Amanda accepted a glass of Champagne from a passing waiter. And as she did, Jack noticed that her hand shook just a little. But there was no other indication whatsoever that she was nervous. She was a thoroughbred to her core, and unlike some of her old co-stars, she looked both beautiful and distinguished. "You look incredible, Amanda," he said, hoping he didn't sound too pushy, but it was hard not to notice her looks anywhere, even in a crowd like this one. And amidst the sequin dresses and holiday satins, her well-cut navy wool dress and sapphire earrings made her look even more spectacular than they did. "Have you been well?" he asked politely.

She hesitated for only a moment. "More or less," she said honestly, with a sad smile. "It's been a pretty rough year. Looking back, I guess I'm just lucky I survived it." And she meant it.

"I went through that once," he said thoughtfully, thinking suddenly of Dori. It was the second time that Amanda had made him think of her, more due to the circumstances than to any physical resemblance, or maybe it was just a feeling.

"I thought you were divorced," Amanda said, looking confused as people all around the room recognized her and pointed discreetly . . . look . . . over there . . . it's Amanda Robbins . . . is she in a movie? . . . haven't seen her in years . . . she looks fabulous . . . do you think she's had a facelift? . . . still great-looking . . . The room was buzzing, although she seemed oblivious to it. She had enormous presence and poise.

"I was divorced," Jack said quietly, explaining his comment to her. In his dark suit, standing next to her, he looked almost like her escort. "But a close friend of mine died thirteen years ago. It wasn't quite the same as what you went through, but it was pretty rugged. She was a very special person."

"I'm sorry," Amanda said gently, with eyes that touched his like matchsticks igniting something that almost frightened him when he felt it. Behind the cool facade, she was a powerful and very magnetic woman. And oddly, after her agonizing year, she looked much more alive to him than when she had been with Matthew. But before he could say anything more to her, he got called away to solve some minor problem with the guest list. Two major stars had just turned up at the door, and had not been invited. He told the security guards at the door to let them in, and then got pulled away for something else by Gladdie. And by then, Jan had come to check on her mother.

"How are you doing, Mom? Are you okay?" She hoped she wasn't ready to leave yet. Jan thought it was good for her to be there, and besides, it was a terrific party.

"I'm fine, sweetheart. Thank you for bringing me. I haven't seen some of these people in years, and Jack has been very pleasant." It was almost an apology for the things she had said about him for the past three years, but he seemed much more respectable to her than he had before, and very comfortable on his own turf. She would have hated to admit it, but she almost liked him. "When's Paul coming?"

"Any minute, I hope. He was in a meeting." And shortly after that, Jan got called to the phone by Gladdie. It was Paul, the meeting was taking forever, but he promised that he'd be there as soon as it was over. "You'll never guess who's here," she said, sounding happy and mischievous, and he laughed as he listened. She was in a better mood than she'd been in in weeks and he was happy to hear it. The tension between them had been getting increasingly stressful.

"Knowing my father, it could be anyone. Tom Cruise . . . Madonna . . ."

"Better than that," she smiled as she held the phone, "Amanda Robbins."

"You actually got her to go with you? Good job, kid. I'm proud of you. How's she doing?"

"She knows practically everyone here, and she looks terrific. She combed her hair, put on a little makeup, and presto magic, the movie star returns. I wish I had her looks."

"You've got her beat hands down, baby. Don't ever forget that."

"I love you," she said, touched by what he'd said, whether or not he meant it.

"Just keep my father away from her, if she's looking so great. That's one headache we don't need. She'd never speak to me again, and neither would you."

"I don't think there's any danger of that," Jan laughed at what he'd said. "But he's been very nice to her. The place is mobbed, and he's been pretty busy. They keep getting celebrity crashers."

"Only women, I'm sure. Poor guy, they'll probably eat him alive and tear his suit off . . . life is tough for some of us. That's my daddy. Anyway, sweetheart, I'll be there as soon as I can. Hang in there. I'll call you when I leave the office."

"See you soon." It was the nicest exchange they'd had in weeks, and when she went to look for her mother, she saw that she was talking to Jack again, and decided to leave them alone. It wouldn't be such a bad thing if they could be friends finally, and stop complaining about each other. And from the distance, while they talked, Jan could see that her mother was smiling, and Jack seemed very earnest.

As it turned out, he was telling her about his buying trips in Europe, and how much he disliked Milan and preferred Paris. And they were exchanging experiences at Claridge's in London. The two seemed like old friends as Jan drifted away to chat with someone she knew, and another hour had gone by when Paul called again, but this time he sounded frazzled. The meeting hadn't gone well, and when he'd gone downstairs, he found that his car had been towed, and he had no way to get to the party, other than to call a cab, but he wanted Jan to pick him up, and in exchange, he promised to take her to dinner. It was really too late for him to try to get to the party.

"What about my mom? I can't just leave her here," she said, sounding worried.

"Why don't you have my dad put her in a cab. He might even have a limo or two standing by. He usually does that for big stars who need a ride somewhere. Just ask him."

"Okay, I'll try. But if she has a fit, I'll call you. I may have to take her home. Otherwise, I'll be there in ten minutes."

"Be here," he said firmly. "I've had a stinking afternoon and I want to see you." A nice, quiet dinner somewhere sounded great to her too, and she hoped that her mother would be willing to have Jack put her in a cab or a limo.

When she found them again, still together in a corner of the room, she explained the situation to them, and for an instant her mother looked panicked. But Jack stepped into it before Amanda could say a word to her daughter. "Paul's right. I have two cars right outside. Whenever your mother wants to go home, I'll have one of them drive her. How does that sound to you?" he asked, turning to Amanda, who still looked startled to be deserted by Jan, but she also didn't want to be a burden to her.

"I . . . that's fine . . . actually, you don't have

to do that, Jack. I can take a cab. I'm just a short hop away in Bel Air. I'll call a taxi."

"No," he said quietly but firmly, "you'll take the limo. You shouldn't be riding around at this hour in a taxi." Amanda laughed at his firmness and the attention, and agreed to take the limo. In fact, she began to make noises about leaving, but he looked so disappointed that she was embarrassed, and agreed to stay a little longer. She was actually having a great time. Matthew had always hated parties, and they hardly ever went to any.

Jan kissed her good-bye and went to retrieve her car, and pick up Paul, and Jack kept a paternal eye on Amanda, making sure she had something to drink, a plate of hors d'oeuvres, met his friends, and felt entirely at ease at the party. She was shocked to realize finally that she was one of the last to leave, and it was already eight-thirty.

"How embarrassing . . . you're going to have to kick me out the door to get rid of me," she said apologetically, and extended a hand to shake his, but he insisted on taking her home himself in the limo.

"Don't be silly, Amanda. It's no trouble for me. We're family, besides it's nice to have a chance to chat after all these years. I'm happy to do it." There was no getting him to agree to let her go home alone, and he left Gladdie with all the instructions she needed when he left. The party was over, and the friends he had planned to have dinner with had already left without him. He had told them he might join them later, or not, but not to count on it in case something came up. And he had no other obligations. And once they were in the car, and driving up Rodeo Drive, he asked her casually if she'd like to stop somewhere for a bite to eat, just a hamburger or a salad, it was such a good chance to talk about their children. She hesitated, thinking she really should go home, but she had no one to account to. And she was a little hungry. He made a good point. She had been worried about Jan and Paul lately, and she wondered if he had also noticed something strained between them. Maybe that was why he wanted to have dinner with her. She assumed so, and decided it was a good idea, and gratefully accepted his offer.

He had the driver take them to the Ivy on North Robertson, and knowing him as well as they did, they gave him a quiet corner table. George Christy was there too, with a group of friends, and he waved when he saw Jack, and then his eyes grew wide when he saw that he was with Amanda Robbins.

They ordered pasta and salads, and Jack moved comfortably into the gap in the conversation. As he had at the store, he talked about a wide variety of things, painting, art, travel, literature, the theater. He was amazingly well informed and pleasant to talk to, and she realized very quickly that he was not the masher she had thought him. And then finally, when the food came, he brought up the subject of their children.

"Do you think they're okay?" He looked concerned, but he seemed perfectly at ease with her. They seemed able to talk about any topic.

"I don't know," she said honestly. "I've been worried about them for a while, but I guess I haven't been much help to Jan. I've been so wrapped up in myself for the past year, I feel as though I've failed her as a mother."

"That's nonsense," he said kindly, "this was the time you needed for you. You can't always be there for everyone else. I'm sure she understood that. She's a terrific girl. . . . I just hope Paul is treating her well. She doesn't look happy."

Amanda sighed then, not wanting to break a confidence, but anxious to share what information she had with Paul's father. This was a perfect opportunity for them to help their children. "I don't want to say anything I shouldn't, Jack. But I think she's very upset about not getting pregnant."

"I thought that might be it," he said, looking pensively at Amanda. "Have they been trying that seriously? Paul never tells me."

"From what I understand, for two years now. That can be very depressing."

"Or a lot of fun, depending on how you look at it," he said irreverently, and she laughed in spite of herself, and then they both grew serious again.

"They don't look like they're having fun, although she seemed better tonight than she has in a long time. She looked like a little girl when she left to pick up Paul."

"Maybe she was just relieved to see you feeling better," he said gently, and Amanda nodded.

"Maybe. The last I heard of it, she wanted Paul to go to a specialist earlier this year, and he didn't want to."

"That serious then. That's not good news. Do you think he's gone yet?"

"I don't think so, although I know she has."

"And?"

"I don't know the details," Amanda admitted to him. "But I do know they're not pregnant. Or at least I don't think so."

"They would have told us if it had worked by now. It really is a worrisome problem. I've teased him about it from time to time, insensitive moron that I am . . . and of course now I realize that I shouldn't have. I wonder if I can broach it with him." He looked pensive.

"I think he worries a lot about his business," Amanda said fairly. She had grown very fond of Paul in the past three years, just as Jack had of her daughter. They were both nice people.

"Paul worries about everything," Jack said with a worried frown. "He's just that kind of person, that's why he's good at what he does, and he's going to be a major player in the film industry one day. Unlike his father, who produced some of the worst movies you've ever seen. Surpassed only by the ones in which I acted. I'm a lot better at women's dresses."

"I'm sure you're being modest about the films,"

Amanda laughed, and then told him how much she liked the store. "It's beautiful, Jack. I'll have to come back one afternoon to go shopping." She liked what she had seen there, and much to her surprise, she liked him too. He was intelligent and interesting and fun to be with. The evening had gone very quickly. And as they left the restaurant, he promised her that he would talk to Paul about going to a specialist with Jan.

"He may not appreciate my talking to him about it, but I'll give it a try."

"I'd really appreciate that," she said gratefully as they got back into the limo.

"I'll let you know how it works out," he promised. "Just think, if we play our cards right, we might be grandparents again by this time next year. Now, there's a thought. I'm turning sixty right after Christmas. That's bad enough without adding more grandchildren . . . for a man like me, that could absolutely destroy my reputation." She liked the way he made light of it, and she couldn't help laughing about it with him, and then for a serious moment, he talked to her again about Dori, how much she had meant to him, and the fact that he had never wanted to be seriously involved with anyone again since then. "It's just too painful," he said honestly. "I don't want to care that much again about anyone, but my children. When the women in my life leave, I want to wave good-bye and forget them. Not cry for two years and remember them for the rest of my life with sorrow. I can't bring myself to do that."

"Maybe the right person hasn't come along again, Jack," she said quietly, thinking of Matthew. She couldn't imagine loving anyone again either, and she said so.

"It's different for you," he said sensibly, "you were married for twenty-six years. You haven't been using up your tickets all over the place the way I have. I've just been having fun, and that's all I want. You should have a life with someone else, if that's what you want, after you've looked around for a while," he said gently. "You haven't been out here in a long time. You may find you actually enjoy it."

"I doubt that," she said honestly. "I can't even imagine dating again, Jack. Not after all these years. I think I'm past that."

"You never know what will happen in life, or who'll come along. Somehow life gives us gifts when we least expect them—or a good kick in the behind. Either one. But it's never what you were expecting."

She nodded, smiling at what he had said, there was a certain truth to it, and then she looked at Jack with a question. "What was Paul's mother like?" She had met her briefly at the wedding, but it had been hard to tell, there had been so much going on, so many guests, so many important details.

"Barbara?" He looked surprised at the question. "She was a monster. Actually, she was the one who cured me from ever wanting to be married, and I'm sure she would tell you the same thing about me, if you asked her. Except of course that she was foolish enough to remarry. I can hardly remember being married to her anymore, fortunately. She left me nineteen years ago. Next year, I'm planning to celebrate the twentieth anniversary of my independence." They were both laughing as he said it.

"Jack Watson, you are awful and irreverent. I bet if the right woman came along you'd marry her in a minute. You're just too busy chasing starlets and models to find her."

"How would you know?" he asked, feigning innocence, but convincing no one, certainly not Amanda.

"I read the papers," she said smugly, and he had the grace to look embarrassed for an instant.

"Well, however that may be, I can assure you that if I met Mrs. Right or Miss Right, I would head for the tallest building and leap to the street immediately. I've learned my lesson. I'm being honest with you, Amanda. I couldn't do it."

"That's how I feel now, although for different reasons. Oh well, it's not a problem I have to face for the moment," she said with a small sigh as they reached her front door and she turned to thank him. "I had a lovely time, Jack, thank you for taking such good care of me, and taking me to dinner to talk about the children." He looked a little startled when she said it, and then he smiled and nodded.

"I'll call and tell you what Paul says," he reiterated, and she thanked him again, unlocked her door, went inside, and closed it behind her. She heard the limo drive away as she turned on the light, and was surprised to realize how wrong she had been about him. He was a womanizer certainly, and he made no secret of it, and yet there was far more to him than that. There was something oddly endearing about him, like a young boy gone wild, but with a look in his eyes that made you want to hug him.

For an instant, it almost made warning bells go off in her head. Men like Jack were dangerous, even for fifty-year-old widows, and yet she knew she had nothing to fear from him. He had his chorus line of women, and all they really had in common was their children. But as Jack rode back to Rodeo Drive to check that the store had been properly put to bed, he sat back against the seat and closed his eyes, and all he could see in his mind's eye was Amanda.

Chapter Four

Amanda didn't hear from Jan for the next few days, and Jack called her a week after the party. He said he had something to tell her, and invited her to come to the store, and have lunch with him in his office. And she accepted without any hesitation. She knew full well that his only motive in calling her was to talk about their children.

He was waiting for her downstairs when she arrived and ushered her upstairs to his private office, where lunch had been set up for them with a starched white tablecloth and napkins on the conference room table. They were left alone, and ate lobster salad and caviar and drank Champagne. It was a very elegant little luncheon.

"Do you do this every day?" she asked, teasing

him, and he said only when he wanted to impress someone. "Then consider me impressed, because I am. I eat yogurt every day out of the container."

"Well, it seems to work. You have an incredible figure, Amanda." She blushed at what he said, and then they moved on to talk about their children. He said he had had lunch with Paul, and had brought the subject up casually, as casually as one could bring up a subject like that one. He had inquired about why they hadn't gotten around to having children, and Jack said that Paul had been pretty candid about it, and told him much the same thing as Amanda. He had also admitted that he really didn't want to go to a doctor about it. Paul thought it was embarrassing, and he felt as though his manhood and virility were being questioned. But after a lengthy conversation with his father, he had finally agreed to do something about it, even though he didn't want to. He had promised to go to the doctor with Jan right after Christmas. Apparently, her doctor was on vacation until then.

"So I would say, our mission has been accomplished. The first stage of it anyway. Operation Grandchild is in its early stages."

Amanda was impressed with how good the results had been, and the fact that he had cared enough to do it, and she sat back in her chair and smiled at him in amazement. "Jack Watson, you are terrific. I can't believe it. Poor Jan has been begging him to go with her for the last year, and he wouldn't do it."

"He's probably just afraid of me. I told him I'd disinherit him if he didn't." He smiled at her, pleased by her reaction. She was so obviously grateful to him.

"Seriously, Jack, thank you. Poor Jan wants a baby so badly."

"What do you suppose will happen if they can't?" He looked worried as he asked her, and she looked concerned too, since Jan had told her that Paul was not in favor of adoption.

"I guess they'll have to face this thing one step at a time. They can always adopt if they don't conceive, but it's hard to believe that in this day and age, with all the fancy methods they use to resolve infertility, they couldn't help them. I'm sure something good will come from all this, with a little patience."

"Things are so damn complicated now, aren't they? In my day, if you were really lucky, it took you six months to get some girl in the back of your dad's car at the drive-in movie, and if you so much as shook hands with her, she got pregnant. Now everyone is being treated for infertility and having babies made in a petri dish, it sure takes the fun out of dating." Amanda couldn't help laughing at what he said. It was true, even in her marriage to Matt, she had frequently worried about getting pregnant. She just hoped that Paul and Jan got lucky now, and managed to have a baby. "I'll keep you posted if I hear anything further," Jack promised.

"So will I," Amanda assured him, and then he

offered to walk around the store with her. She couldn't resist trying a few things, and he finally left her with the manager of the store and the best of their sales force, and she showed up in his office to thank him again two hours later.

"Did you have fun?" he asked her, as he stood up at his desk when she walked in the room. She looked happy and relaxed and she had had a great time shopping at Julie's.

"I had a ball, and I bought everything in sight, including half a dozen really great bathing suits for next summer from your cruise line." She had also bought several beautiful nightgowns, a new dress, and a sensational black alligator handbag. "I bought everything in sight," she said again, with a degree of embarrassment. "I haven't been this extravagant ever in my life, but I have to admit I enjoyed it." She laughed as she confessed, and he found himself staring at how beautiful she was, and wondering how he could get her to have dinner with him.

"Do you like Thai food?" he suddenly asked her out of nowhere.

"Why, do you sell that too? Is there a department I missed? A deli?" She was laughing at him, and she looked sensual and young and happy.

"Yes, actually, I'll show you where it is," he said convincingly. "But it's at our other store, and you have to come in my car to get there."

"Oh, you're a terrible liar, Jack Watson. You're

trying to kidnap me and hold me for ransom, I just know it."

"What a good idea," he said, laughing with her. "What are my chances?"

"Now? Tonight?" It was already five-thirty, but the store was open till nine so their customers could shop for Christmas. "You gave me lunch today, you don't have to feed me tonight too. I have another idea. Why don't you come out to the house a little later on, and I'll cook you dinner. Nothing fancy, just whatever I find in the fridge, more or less. I owe you one, a big one, for getting Paul to go to the doctor."

"I'd love it." He accepted her invitation instantly, and promised to be there at seven o'clock to help her. And as soon as she left, he picked up the phone and canceled the date that he had set up weeks before for that evening. He claimed to have the flu, and the girl he called just laughed at him. She didn't really care, but she knew him a lot better than he suspected.

"What's her name?" The girl he had called couldn't resist a little teasing.

"What makes you think it's another woman?"

"Because you're not gay, and you probably haven't had the flu since you were two. You sound fine to me, Jack . . . good luck with whoever she is." She was seeing someone else anyway, and he thanked her for being so understanding.

He arrived at Amanda's door at exactly seven

o'clock, and she was wearing a pair of gray slacks with a pale blue sweater set and a string of pearls. She looked like a young heiress, but she was wearing an apron.

"Very domestic picture," he commented as he came in and set down a bottle of very fancy wine he had bought for her, and she laughed at his comment.

"I hope so, after twenty-six years of marriage."

"You know, I never thought of you that way before, domestic I mean," Jack confessed as he followed her into the kitchen and she thanked him for the wine. It was an excellent wine, and an impressive vintage. "I only thought of you in terms of being a movie star. It's hard to forget who you were before. You even look the same. In fact, in my mind, I always think of you as Amanda Robbins, and not Amanda Kingston."

"Matt hated that," she said simply. "A lot of people used to say that."

"Is that why you never went back?" He was curious about her.

"Probably. Matt wouldn't have wanted me to anyway. We talked about it a lot before we got married. I hadn't been at it long, but I was ready to give it up . . . for something better . . . a man I loved and a family."

"And was it better? Were you happy?" he asked, as he watched her.

"I loved being with my kids, and with Matt. It was a good life." She looked pensive for a moment then, as she thought about it. "It's hard to believe that it's over. Everything shattered so quickly. One minute he was leaving the house with his tennis racket in his hand, and the next he was gone, just two hours later. It's hard to adjust to."

Jack nodded. "It sounds dumb to say it, but at least he didn't suffer."

"I guess that's true, but we did. I wasn't prepared at all. He seemed so young. We never even talked about what would happen if one of us died. We never had time to think about it, or say good-bye, or . . ." Tears filled her eyes and she turned away, and suddenly Jack was behind her, holding her shoulders.

"It's okay . . . I know . . . that's how it was for me with Dori. She had a car accident on the way to meet me. Head-on. She never knew what hit her. But I did. I felt like that goddamn truck had hit me. For a long time, I wished it would have. I kept wanting it to be me, and not her . . . I felt so damn guilty."

"So did I," Amanda said as she turned to look at him. He had kind eyes, they were a warm brown, and his hair was a sandy blonde peppered with gray. He was astonishingly good-looking. "For the last year, I kept wishing I had died instead of Matt. But for the last week or two, I'm suddenly glad I didn't. I've been enjoying my kids again, and doing little things. . . . It's funny how things change just the smallest bit, and it makes a difference." He nodded, and put on one of her aprons over the slacks and black turtleneck sweater he was wearing.

"Okay, enough of this serious stuff, madam. What's for dinner? Do you want me to chop, grate, or puree, or would you rather just watch me get quietly drunk in your kitchen? I can do either." She laughed at him as he looked at her with amusement. It was so easy to be with him.

"Why don't you sit and relax. Everything is pretty much done already." She poured him a glass of wine, did a few things in the kitchen, and half an hour later, they had steak, baked potatoes, and salad. She was a good cook, and they talked for hours, sitting at her kitchen table, and afterward they walked into the living room and he glanced at some of the pictures. They were a handsome family, though Matt always looked stiff to him, but Amanda looked lovely in every picture.

"It's a shame you and your daughters are so ugly."

"Your kids are just as good-looking as mine," she complimented him, and he laughed.

"We just happen to be extremely attractive people. Everyone in Los Angeles is. They make the ugly people move to some other state, or town, or ship them over the border at midnight. They just round them up and off they go and no one ever sees them again . . . poof . . . no more ugly people." He liked to play with her, and tease. It was easy to see why he had so much success with women.

"Don't you get tired of it?" she asked him honestly as they sat down. She felt as though she could ask him anything. They were friends now. "All the women, I mean. I would think it would be exhausting to be with strangers all the time. I can't even imagine having to deal with it, starting all over again constantly, asking all those tedious questions. . . ."

"Stop!" He put up a hand with a groan. "You're destroying my lifestyle. If you make me question it, I may not be able to do it. It's just one way of never getting involved. That's all. It's what I've needed ever since Dori."

"I'd rather watch TV, or read a book," Amanda said honestly, and he laughed.

"Well, actually . . . that could be the essence of the difference between men and women. Up until now, if the choice was book, TV, or women, I would have to pick women. But if you make me think about it with any seriousness, I may have to buy myself a new TV set tomorrow morning."

"You're hopeless."

"I am. It used to be part of my charm, but I can see that it's rapidly becoming a liability. Maybe we shouldn't discuss this."

They talked about other things then, their families when they were young, their dreams, their ambitions, their careers, and once again their children. And the night flew by again. It was after midnight when he finally left her. And not quite nine o'clock when he called her the next morning to thank her for dinner. She was still sleeping.

"Did I wake you?" He seemed surprised. She looked like one of those early-rising people, and normally she was, but she had stayed up late the night before, trying to read, and thinking about him.

"No, not at all. I was up," she lied, looking at the clock and surprised at what time it was. She had a dentist appointment to have her teeth cleaned, and she was about to miss it.

"You're lying," he said with a grin at his end. "You were sound asleep and I woke you. The life of the indolent rich. I've been at my desk since eight-thirty." He had had a number of calls to make to Europe, where it was nine hours later. But she had been preying on his mind, and he had decided to call her on the spur of the moment. And now, hearing her, he was unexpectedly nervous. "How about dinner tonight?" he asked without preamble, and her eyes opened wide, wondering if she had heard him correctly.

"Tonight?" She had nothing planned, although the following day she had been invited to a Christmas party. "I . . . aren't you going to get tired of me?"

"I don't think that's possible, and we have a lot to catch up on, don't we?"

"Like what?" She lay on her back and stretched, remembering exactly what he looked like.

"Both our lives. Between us that covers a hundred and ten years, it could take a while, and I figured we really ought to get started, though we made some good inroads last night."

"Is this how you do it?" she smiled. "All that charm? A hundred and ten years . . . what a way to think about it. Well, all right, as long as you put it that way, we'd better do it. What did you have in mind?"

"How about dinner at L'Orangerie? I'll pick you up at seven-thirty."

"Sounds wonderful. I'll be ready." But as soon as she hung up, she panicked. She sat up in bed and stared across the bedroom she had shared for twenty-six years with her husband. What in God's name was she doing? Was she playing Girl of the Hour with Jack Watson? How stupid was she? She got out of bed and decided to call him to cancel. But as soon as she called, Gladdie told her he had gone into a meeting, but she could leave him a message. But it seemed so rude to just leave him a message saying she couldn't have dinner with him, so she said that it was nothing important.

He called her back at noon anyway, and when she answered the phone, he sounded worried. "Anything wrong? Are you okay?" He actually sounded as though it mattered to him, which was even more unnerving.

"I'm fine . . . I just thought . . . oh, I don't know, Jack, I was just feeling stupid. I don't want to be the Flavor of the Month. I'm a married woman, or at least I was . . . or I still am . . . in my own mind, and I don't know what the hell I'm doing with you, or what game I'm playing. I can't even bring myself to take off my wedding band, and now I'm having dinner with you every night, and I have no idea where this is going." She looked and felt exhausted when she finished talking, and at his end, he sounded calm, although he didn't feel it.

"I don't know where this is going either. And if it'll make you feel any better, I'll buy a wedding band too, and then at least we'll be even. People will think we're both cheating on our spouses. I just know I enjoy your company more than I've enjoyed anyone in years, maybe ever. And I can't tell you more than that. All of a sudden, the life I've led for twenty years looks like a bad joke in the back of *Playboy*. I'm embarrassed by it, I want to get rid of it, and God help me for saying this, but I want to be the kind of person you'd be proud to be seen with, because I'm so damn proud to be with you, I can't stand it."

"But I'm not ready for a relationship," she said mournfully. "I don't want to start dating. It's only been a year since I lost Matt, and I don't know what I'm doing with you . . . but I love talking to you too . . . and I don't want to stop, but maybe we should. Do you think we should cancel dinner tonight? Do you think this is wrong?" She sounded so worried that he just wanted to put his arms around her and hug her.

"It's going to be all right," he said gently, "we're not going to do anything you don't like. We'll just talk about our kids, and relax. It doesn't have to be more than that for now . . . or maybe ever." It cost him dearly to say that, but he didn't want to frighten her, or worse yet, to lose her, before he even won her over. Suddenly it all mattered to him greatly. And then he had another thought. "Maybe we should go somewhere a little less public for dinner. . . ." L'Orangerie was one of the best restaurants in L.A., and they were bound to be seen there. "What about some little bistro, or even a pizza?"

"That sounds terrific, Jack. And I'm sorry I'm such a lunatic. I just wasn't expecting us to be friends, or not like this anyway . . . whatever this is." She laughed nervously and he tried to reassure her.

"I'll pick you up. You can wear jeans, if you want."

"Great." She took him at his word, and when he arrived, she was wearing faded jeans wallpapered to her spectacular body and a big cozy pink angora sweater. He was dying to tell her how great she looked, but he didn't want to scare her.

They drove to La Cienega, and they stopped at a little restaurant she had never even seen before. They were talking animatedly as they walked in, and suddenly she clutched his arm, and turned away with a look of terror.

"What is it?" If she had been married, he would have guessed that she had just seen her husband in the corner, with another woman. All he could see was a young couple dining there, but Amanda was already out the door, and her heart was pounding. "Who was that?"

"My daughter Louise and her husband, Jerry."

"Oh my God. That's all right. Aren't we allowed to be eating dinner? We both have our clothes on." He tried to make light of it, but she looked as though she wanted to run away, and he didn't want that to happen. They walked back to his car, and talked for a moment once they were safely inside it.

"She'd never understand it."

"She's a grown woman, for heaven's sake. What do your kids expect? For you to stay home for the rest of your life? I'm Jan's father-in-law, I'm harmless." He tried to look innocent, but this time Amanda laughed at him.

"You are anything but harmless, and you know it. And my kids think you're a masher."

"That's nice. I hope Jan doesn't think that . . . well, come to think of it, maybe she does. I guess for quite a while now, I've been one. But there's always the possibility that I might reform. Would that count?"

"No. And certainly not tonight. Maybe I should go home."

"Tell you what, we'll go to Johnny Rocket." She smiled at the suggestion. It was where the kids hung out, drinking milkshakes and eating hamburgers, just like they did in the fifties.

And when they got there, they sat at the counter and ate chili dogs and fries, and drank milkshakes, and Amanda even managed to laugh at herself, before they ordered coffee.

"Did I look like a complete fool running out of there?" She looked like a kid who had made a huge faux pas, and couldn't believe she'd done it, but Jack loved everything about her.

"No. You looked like a married woman out on a date, who had just seen her husband."

"That's what I felt like," she confessed with a sigh, and then glanced up at him. "Jack, I'm not up to this. Honestly, I'm not. I think you should go back to the chorus line again, you're a lot better off with them, believe me."

"I think you should let me decide that." And then out of nowhere, he asked her what she was doing the following week for Christmas.

"The kids are coming to my house on Christmas Eve, they do every year. And then this year we're going to Louise's on Christmas Day. Why? What do you do?"

"Sleep, usually. . . . I mean, as in snoring, nothing more exotic than that. Christmas in the retail business is a nightmare. We're open till midnight on Christmas Eve, to accommodate our customers who can't face their shopping until nine o'clock that night, mostly husbands. It's as if they lose their calendars every year and find them at six o'clock on Christmas Eve. . . . Oh my God, it's Christmas! I usually take the last shift and then I go home and sleep for two days. It works for me, but I was just wondering if you wanted to go skiing with me the day after. You know, separate rooms, just good friends and all that."

"I don't think I should. What if someone sees me? It hasn't been a year yet."

"When will that be?" He honestly couldn't remember.

"On the fourth of January," she said solemnly, "and I'm actually not much of a skier."

"It was just an idea, I thought it might do you good, to get some fresh air, and get away. We could drive up to Lake Tahoe, or stop in San Francisco."

"Maybe someday," she said vaguely, and he nodded. He was pushing it, and he knew it. She really wasn't ready.

"Don't worry about it. Why don't you drop by the store one of these days. I'll be there all week, and we can eat caviar in my office." She smiled at the suggestion. In spite of his reputation, and the fact that she wasn't ready for this, she really liked him. And he seemed to understand everything that she was feeling. There was a warm, caring side to him, that had taken her by surprise and caught her off guard completely. And he seemed so much younger than Matt, so full of life, so happy to be with her, and much as she didn't want to feel that way about him, she found that she loved being with him.

They talked about it that night, in the car, on the way home, and he confessed that she was not at all what he had expected her to be, once he got to know her. She was funny and warm and kind and compassionate, and so vulnerable. Everything she said or did, made him want to protect her.

"Can you stand just being friends for a while," she asked him honestly, "or maybe even forever? I don't know that I'll ever want to get involved again. I'm just not sure I could ever do that."

"No one's asking you to make that decision," he said sanely, and she calmed down and stopped feeling quite as guilty. He came in for a while, and they drank mint tea in her kitchen, and then eventually he lit a fire in the living room, and they talked for a long time about the things that were important to them.

It was two o'clock when he left, and she didn't know where the night had gone. The hours seemed to fly by when they were together. The next morning he was busy at the store, and she spent the day doing all the last-minute details of getting ready for Christmas. She had already bought the tree, and she was decorating it that night when he called her.

"What are you doing?" he asked, sounding tired. He had been at the store for twelve hours, and he was exhausted.

"Decorating the tree," she said, but she sounded sad, and she had put carols on the stereo, which suddenly seemed even sadder. It was her first Christmas without Matt, her first as a widow.

"Do you want me to come by? I'm leaving the

store in half an hour, and you're on my way home. I'd love to see you."

"I don't think we should," she said honestly. She still needed time to mourn, and this was one of those private moments. Instead, they talked for a while, and when they hung up, she felt a little better, and he felt worse, and suddenly desperately lonely. He wondered if she was ever going to let go of Matt, or be ready to let someone in behind her walls. He knew that he had glimpsed into her heart, but she was still afraid to let him approach her, and maybe she always would be.

Jack drove slowly past her house on the way home, and he could see the lights blinking on the tree inside, but he couldn't see her. She was sitting in her bedroom, crying, because she was desperately afraid she was falling in love with Jack and she didn't want to. It wasn't fair to Matt, and more than anything, she didn't want to betray him. After twenty-six years she owed him more than that, more than just falling for the first man who came along, no matter how charming he was. And what would happen if she did turn out to be one of the girls in his chorus line? She would have cheapened herself for nothing. And she knew with absolute certainty that, for Matt's sake, and her own, she couldn't let that happen.

Jack called her when he got home, but she didn't answer the phone. She knew instinctively that it was him, and she didn't want to talk to him. She wanted to end this even before it happened.

She turned out the lights that night, and went to bed, and left the music on, and the strains of "Silent Night" drifted through the house as she cried, for two men, one she had loved for so long, and the other she would never know. It was hard to tell at that exact moment which pain was greater, and which of them she most longed for.

Chapter Five

Jack only called her once or twice over the next few days. He could sense what was happening to her, and he knew how hard it was for her over the holidays. Dori had died in November, and he had stayed drunk for an entire week between Christmas and New Year's.

He wisely left Amanda alone to cope with her feelings privately, but on the morning of Christmas Eve, he had a Christmas gift dropped off for her. It was a small eighteenth-century sketch of an angel that she had admired in the store, and it was very pretty. He wrote a brief note to go with it, and told her that he hoped an angel would be watching over her, this Christmas and always. He signed it "Jack," and she was deeply touched when she saw it, and a little while later she called to thank him. She sounded more distant than before, but a lot calmer. She was obviously coming to terms with whatever it was she was feeling. And although he was happy to hear from her, he was careful not to frighten her by being too intimate with her. But right now he was totally swallowed up by the store anyway. They had had a few problems, a small theft, a nearly fatal heart attack the day before, and a small army of lost children. The usual crises over Christmas. They had also lost the gold sequined dress of a famous star, and then found it miraculously, and had had two famous women slugging it out over one man, in cosmetics. The holidays had not been without excitement.

"I hope you have a good time with your kids tonight, though I know it will be hard for you without Matt."

"He always carved the turkey," she said sadly. She sounded so small suddenly, and all he wanted to do was put his arms around her.

"Have Paul do it," Jack said gently. "I taught him everything I know. About turkeys, not about women." She smiled at what he said, and asked him if there was any news about Paul. Jack told her that Paul had an appointment to go to the specialist between Christmas and New Year's. "I hope everything checks out fine," Jack said hopefully.

"So do I," she agreed with him, and she suddenly wished she had invited him to dinner, but the children would have wondered why he was there, and he couldn't have left the store anyway, and what point was there in asking him? She wasn't going to pursue a relationship with him. She had already made that decision, and as he sat listening to her on the phone, from his desk, Jack could hear her decision about him in her tone. She had already taken a definite distance from him. He thought about calling someone to go out with him on New Year's Eve, but for once in his life, he didn't even want to. He had already made reservations to go to Tahoe the day after Christmas, and he was going alone.

"Merry Christmas, Amanda," he said gently before they hung up, and he sat in his office for a long time, thinking about her. He had never known anyone like her.

And that night, as he walked around the store, helping out wherever he was needed, he thought about them eating turkey at her house, the children, and the tree, his own son, and her two daughters, and he suddenly realized what a wasteland his life was. He had spent the last ten years chasing tits and cute little asses in tight blue jeans, and what had it gotten him? Absolutely nothing.

"You don't look like you're having such a good Christmas," Gladdie said when she left that night. He had given her a beautiful cashmere coat, and an enormous bonus. "Something wrong? The kids okay?" She worried about him, and she knew there was no hot mama of the moment. She also knew that he had called Paul's mother-in-law several times, and she was afraid that he might be sick, or something might be wrong with the marriage, but Jack had purposely said nothing about it.

"No, I'm fine," he lied. Except that I've wasted my life, the only woman I ever loved died thirteen years ago, and the best woman I've ever met before or since wants to bury herself with her husband. No big deal, Gladdie. Merry Christmas. "Just tired, I guess. Christmas in this business is a killer."

"Every year I tell myself we'll never get through it, but we do," she smiled. Financially, it had been their best year ever.

"So what are you doing tonight?" He smiled at her as she put her new coat on. It was a soft lavender-blue and she loved it.

"Sleeping with my husband. Literally. The poor guy hasn't seen me awake in six weeks, and he probably won't for another week."

"You should take a couple of days off. You deserve it."

"Maybe when you're in Tahoe." But he knew she wouldn't. She never did. She was the only human being he knew who worked harder than he did.

As he did every year, he worked until after midnight, and he was with the night watchman when they finally locked up at one o'clock in the morning.

"Merry Christmas, Mr. Watson."

"Thanks, Harry. Same to you." He waved, and slid slowly into his red Ferrari. But he was too tired to sleep when he got home. He watched television for a while, and thought about calling someone, but by then it was three o'clock in the morning. And for some odd reason, he felt as though those days were over. He just didn't care anymore. There were no legs long enough, no breasts big enough, no skin soft enough to woo him.

"Christ, maybe I'm dying," he said out loud, and then laughed to himself as he went to bed. Maybe turning sixty was doing it, and not just Amanda. There was no fool like an old fool, and he had certainly been one.

He slept until noon the next day, and thought about calling her, but when he did, she was already gone. She was at Louise's house with her family, eating yet another turkey. He drove out to north L.A. and picked up some Chinese food instead, and then sat on his unmade bed, eating it, and watching football. He called a couple of girls after that, and wanted to ask them out for dinner that night, but everyone was out, and he was actually relieved not to reach them.

He knew Amanda was home that night, but he didn't call. What could he say to her? Are you over your husband yet? Suddenly he felt like a fool for badgering her, and he tossed and turned all night, and thought of her. And finally, the next morning, he couldn't stand it. He was leaving for Tahoe that afternoon, but when she answered the phone he asked her if he could come by for a cup of coffee.

She sounded surprised, and a little worried, but she invited him over anyway. There was always the possibility that he wanted to talk to her about Paul, or Jan, but she didn't think so. And when she saw his face, when she opened the door to him at one o'clock, she knew that it had nothing to do with their children.

"You look tired," she said, looking concerned about him.

"I am. I can't sleep anymore. Turning sixty is rougher than I thought," he said with a wry smile. "I think I'm finally losing my marbles."

"How's that?" He followed her inside, and they walked into her comfortable kitchen. She had a pot of coffee on, and offered him a cup, and then they sat down at her kitchen table.

He looked at her over his coffee and asked her bluntly, "I've made a real nuisance of myself, haven't I? I guess mashers don't clean up all that well. I got a little overexcited. I'm sorry if I made you uncomfortable, that was never my intention." He looked desperately unhappy as he said it, and a lot less than sixty. He looked and felt like a kid again, visiting the one girl in the class who didn't want to go steady with him. "I know how hard this time is for you. I'm sorry if I made it any harder for you."

"You didn't, Jack," she said gently, her eyes boring into his, she looked as unhappy as he felt, and as though she felt so desperately torn that she didn't know what to do about it. "I know I shouldn't say this to you, but I've missed you." While he pretended to look calm, his heart flipped over as she said it.

"You have? When?"

"For the past few days. I've missed talking to you, and seeing you. I honest to God don't know what I'm doing."

"Neither do I. I've been feeling like an utter fool, and the biggest pain in the ass that ever lived. I've been trying to leave you alone, because I figured that was what you wanted."

"I did." But there was a catch in her voice as she said it.

"And now?" He held his breath as he waited.

"I don't know." She looked up at him with eyes the color of a cameo and all he wanted to do was kiss her, but he knew he couldn't.

"Just take your time. You don't need to make any decisions. Go slow. I'm here. I'm not going anywhere. . . ." And then he remembered, with a grin. "Except Lake Tahoe."

"Now?" She smiled at him, she really liked being with him.

"Later. I still have to go home and pack my ski clothes. I should have packed yesterday, but I was too beat to do it." She nodded then, and they talked, and a little while later, they were comfortable again, and she was laughing at him. He was describing the incident in the store when the two women got into a fistfight over their common boyfriend.

"Can you imagine what the tabloids would have done with that? And of course, if they got hold of it, both women would have blamed us for squealing. Actually, they deserved it." He still hadn't told her who they were, and said he wouldn't. He was surprisingly discreet about his business. "So what are you going to do this week?"

"Nothing much. Maybe I'll see the kids, if they're not too busy." But he didn't reiterate his invitation to Lake Tahoe. He knew she just wasn't ready. "Maybe I'll go to a movie. What about you? Are you taking anyone with you?" She was still trying to convince herself they were just friends, and it wouldn't bother her in the least if he was taking a woman along, but it would have, and she knew it.

"No, I'm going alone. I ski better that way." And then, tired of playing games with her, he took her hand in his and held it. "I'm going to miss you." She nodded and said nothing, and then she looked at him, and she would have melted him to his soul if he'd been wearing asbestos. "What are you doing on New Year's Eve?" he asked casually, and she laughed at him.

"Same thing I do every year. Matthew hated New Year's Eve. We went to bed at ten o'clock every year, and wished each other a Happy New Year the next morning."

"Sounds exciting." He smiled.

"What about you?" she asked with interest.

"Mine will be about like yours this year. I might stay up at Tahoe." And then as he looked at her, he felt suddenly stupid. "On the other hand, Amanda, . . . we could do something a little different. We could hang around together here. Just as friends, and go to movies and watch television together. I don't have to go to work, and there's no law that says we can't be friends, is there?"

"What about your ski trip?"

"I have a bum knee anyway." He grinned. "My orthopedist would thank you."

"And then what? I mean after that . . . that's the part that scares me." Oddly enough, she found it easy to be honest with him.

"We don't have to worry about that part yet. No one's keeping score here. We have a right not to be alone over the holidays. Who are we proving what to? You? Me? Our kids? Matt? It's been a year. You paid your dues. If nothing else, we have a right to a little comfort and friendship. How much trouble can we get into at a movie?" He was very convincing.

"With you? Probably more than I dare to think of."

"I'll sit alone in the back row. I won't even come near you."

"You're crazy." She shook her head as she looked at him, trying to will herself to say no to him, to send him away, she knew she should, but everything about him was so damnably appealing.

"I came to the same conclusion myself yesterday—that I'm crazy. Actually, it almost had me worried."

"Me too," she laughed again. "Everything about you has me worried. If I had any sense, I'd tell you that I don't want to see you again until the christening of Paul and Jan's first baby."

"That could be a while. Even at best, we're talking nine months. That's a long time to forgo movies. So what do you say?"

"I say go to Lake Tahoe, and have a great time, Jack. Call me when you get back sometime."

"Okay," he said. He was old enough and wise enough to know when he wasn't going to win. It killed him to leave her, but he got up, wishing that he could convince her. "Happy New Year," he said, as he kissed the top of her head and walked out of her kitchen. He was already at the front door, and had opened it, when he heard her say something, and he turned around and saw her standing in the kitchen doorway. "What did you just say?" The look in her eyes rooted him to the spot. She looked frightened, but strong, and her eyes never left him.

"I said there's a movie I want to see at the Beverly Center. It starts at four, if you want to join me."

"Do you mean that?" His voice was a whisper in the chill hallway.

"I think I do . . . I want to . . . but I don't know yet."

"I'll pick you up at three-thirty. Wear jeans. We'll

go to the Thai place for dinner. Okay?" A slow smile dawned in his eyes as she nodded. And without another word, before she could change her mind again, he drove home to cancel his reservations in Tahoe.

Chapter Six

The next five days were magical. They seemed to hang in space like a time warp. They went to movies, walked in the park, talked about anything that came to mind, or sometimes just sat together, in silence. There seemed to be no pressure on either of them. He called the store, but he didn't go in, and of course Gladdie was there. She hadn't taken time off after all. But for the first time in years, he didn't give a damn about Julie's. He just wanted to be with Amanda. Nothing was said, no questions were asked, no answers were offered, and nothing was promised. They just spent time together. And it was exactly what they both needed and wanted.

It was as though day by day Amanda could feel herself healing. And he felt himself becoming the man he had once been, with Dori, only better. He was older and wiser, and had squandered a lot of time in the last thirteen years. It suddenly seemed to him as though it had been someone else's life, and it no longer mattered.

She talked about Matt sometimes, and once she cried about him, but she seemed to feel more peaceful about him. She was slowly accepting that he had died and she had lived, and she wanted to stop feeling guilty about it. And without saying anything to Jack, she had quietly slipped off her wedding ring, and put it away in her jewel box. She had cried over it, but she no longer felt right wearing it. For the first instant it had slipped off she thought it would tear her heart out. She never mentioned it to Jack. But he saw it immediately the next time they had dinner, and knowing what a big step it must have been for her, he diplomatically made no comment.

They ate some good food, in restaurants all over town, where they saw no one they knew, and they saw some of the worst movies ever made, and then laughed about them. He went back to his own place at night, and they hovered in her doorway for a long time, just talking and saying good night. But it wasn't until the day before New Year's Eve that, without thinking, while she was cooking dinner for him that night, he reached out and pulled her to him and kissed her. He had wanted to do that for so long, and he was suddenly terrified that he would frighten her away again, but she looked anything but afraid as she looked up at him with a slow smile afterward, and he felt relief wash over him. He hadn't lost her. They didn't say anything, but he kissed her again later that night, as they sat in the living room, in the dark, holding hands, and looking at the fire he had lit. She felt completely comfortable with him.

And at midnight he went home, and as soon as he got there, he called her.

"I feel like a kid again, Amanda," he said, and he sounded irresistibly sexy.

"So do I," she smiled. "Thank you for going slow with me. This week has been incredible. It was just what I needed. I just wanted some time with you . . . it's a real gift . . . better than Christmas."

They laughed over the fact that the phone had rung a couple of times that night. They both assumed that it had been her children, but she hadn't answered. She wanted this time for herself, and for him. The children had had their fair share over the years, and so had Matt, and now it was her turn. It was the first time in years she had a life that no one knew about, and that didn't include her family. This was good for her for a change, and she knew it.

They had already planned to go ice-skating the next day, and maybe to another movie. They had seen just about everything in town by then, and they were going to cook dinner on New Year's Eve, and drink Champagne, and try to stay awake until midnight.

"I'm sorry you didn't get to go skiing," she said generously on the phone to him.

"I'm not," he laughed at the idea. "This is a whole lot better. This is the most romantic thing I've ever done in my whole life, and I wouldn't miss it for anything, sure as hell not a bunch of moguls."

He said good night to her, and wished he could kiss her again, and the next day they laughed like two kids when they went skating. They had a great time. And that night, on New Year's Eve, she made roast duck for him, and a soufflé for dessert. It was a perfect dinner.

It was ten o'clock by the time they were in front of the fire again, and he was kissing her, and she was returning his kisses with passion. He poured them each a glass of Champagne, and they drank it faster than they planned. In the warmth of the fire, and the glow of the Champagne, his kisses seemed headier than ever, and she had no idea what time it was when his deep, sexy voice told her that he loved her, and asked her to go to bed with him. She didn't say anything. She only clung to him and nodded. She wanted him more than anything, and for once he couldn't even make himself stop to wonder if she'd regret it. He wanted her too badly. And he followed her into her bedroom. And what he discovered there filled him with wonder, she had a body almost like a girl's, only somehow better. She was long and lean, with fuller breasts than he had expected. He couldn't get enough of her, and she told him she loved him as he entered her, and she could hardly breathe as they moved slowly together. It was something she had never dreamed of or shared before, not with her husband, or the two men who had come before him. For a young girl in Hollywood at the time, she had been surprisingly chaste, but now they brought no history to each other. All they shared was their passion and the present, and when they came, she felt as though the universe had exploded in her head, and her body lay sated beneath him. She loved the noises he made, and the way he touched her, and the feel of him inside her. She was entirely his now, and she fell asleep in his arms soon afterward, long before midnight. There was no sorrow. No regret. And no reckoning. Until the next morning.

She awoke in his arms, as he caressed her breasts, smiling at her, and the sunlight streamed across the room she had shared with her husband. She lay quiet for a long time, and then she looked at Jack, not sure whether to laugh or cry, or make love to him again, and wanting to do all three at the same time. Instead, she slipped slowly out of bed and walked across the room, and then turned to look at him, like a young doe, in all her glory.

"Are you okay?" He watched her, filled with desire for her again, but suddenly worried. She seemed different.

"I'm not sure," she said quietly, and then sat down in a chair, still naked, looking at him, trying to decide if she was crazy, or just very happy. "I can't believe I did that last night." Neither could he, but he had never been happier in his life, and he didn't want to give her up now. He knew who and what she was, and he wanted her desperately. And she had told him she loved him.

"Just don't tell me I got you drunk . . . that will kill me."

"You didn't," she looked at him nervously from underneath cream-colored eyelids, "but was I?" She seemed frightened.

"I don't see how . . . you only had two glasses. . . ."

"It was the fire . . . and you kissing me . . . and . . ."

"Amanda, don't do this. Stop torturing yourself." He walked across the room to her, and knelt next to her, his own body as splendid as hers was.

"I made love to you in the bed I shared with my husband." Tears suddenly filled her eyes as he looked at her, refusing to regret he had done it. "I can't believe I did that. My God, Jack, what kind of woman am I? I was married to the man for twenty-six years, and I made love with you in his bed." She stood up and began pacing, as he tried not to let himself get angry.

"Don't make it sound like a crime, Amanda. You made love to me, and I made love to you. Amanda, . . . I love you. For God's sake, we're grown-ups. You're still alive . . . my God, are you still alive! . . . and I'm more alive than I've been in twenty or thirty years, maybe in my entire lifetime." The phone rang as he said it, and she made no move to answer. She didn't give a damn who was calling. All she could think of now was her betrayal of her husband.

"It's *his* bed. *Our* bed." She was openly crying as he watched her pacing, but he was afraid to touch her.

"Then buy a new one," he exploded at her in spite of himself. "It's *your* bed, for chrissakes. We'll do it on the floor next time . . . or at my place. . . ."

"You'd need an exorcist to purify your bed!" she said in tears, and he laughed at her.

"Sweetheart, calm down . . . please . . . it's just traumatic. It's the first time. I understand that. For chrissake, it's the best sex I ever had . . . we love each other . . . we just spent a week together, and we're crazy about each other. What do you expect? Christ, we saw every rotten movie in town. What more do you want? A two-year engagement?"

"Maybe. He isn't even dead a year yet." She sat down again, and cried like a kid, and all he dared to do was hand her a tissue.

"The anniversary of his death is in three days. We'll wait. We'll forget this ever happened."

"Good. We'll go back to being friends again. We'll go to movies, and we won't have sex again. Ever." She was trying to make it right with herself, but he was only willing to go so far. He loved her too much now to lose any part of her, particularly the parts he had discovered the previous evening. They were pure legend.

"Let's not get crazy about this, shall we? We'll have a cup of coffee, we'll take a shower, and we'll go for a nice long walk, and you'll feel better."

"I'm a whore, Jack. Just like all the other girls you sleep with." The phone rang again, and they both ignored it.

"You are *not* a whore. And I don't sleep with anyone anymore except you. Do you understand that? I haven't looked at another woman since you came to the party at the store. You've ruined it for me, and I'm not going to let you ruin it for us too. We love each other, you have a right to that. Do you get that?"

"I don't have a right to sleep with anyone in my husband's bed." She was distraught, and he was getting exasperated. But he walked over to her, firmly took her hand, and pulled her to her feet.

"Come on, let's get a cup of coffee." Neither of them did anything to cover themselves and it never occurred to her that she was completely unembarrassed with him. It was as though they had been together forever.

He made her a cup of coffee standing naked in her kitchen, and handed it to her. She drank it black, and it burned going down, but she was a little calmer when they sat down together at the kitchen table. The kitchen was warm, and they sat there together, naked and drinking the hot coffee.

"Do you want the paper?" she asked matter-of-factly, suddenly feeling utterly schizophrenic. One moment she was completely at home with him, the next riddled with guilt and anguish. But she was feeling better again now, as he nodded.

"Sure. I'd like to see the paper."

"I'll get it."

She walked to the front door, coffee cup still in hand, opened the front door, and bent down to get the paper. Her front door was completely shielded from sight, and she knew no one would see her. But just as she bent down, she saw Jan's car drive in, and both Jan and Paul stared openmouthed at her. She grabbed the paper, ran inside, slammed the door, and darted into the kitchen, dropping the paper and spilling her coffee. Jack looked at her in amazement.

"You have to leave!" She was staring at him in horror.

"*Now?*"

"Yes . . . oh   shit . . . no,   you   can't . . . they're outside . . . go out the back door . . . it's behind the laundry." She pointed in the general direction, waving frantically at him.

"Do you want me to leave like this? Or can I have a minute to put my clothes on?" But just as he asked the question, the doorbell rang, and Amanda nearly jumped a foot when she heard it.

"Oh my God . . . it's them . . . oh my God . . . Jack, what are we going to do?" She was in tears again, and this time he was laughing.

"Who is it? The Fuller Brush man? It's New Year's Day, for chrissake. Just ignore it."

"It's our *children*, you moron. They *saw* me . . . when I went to get the paper."

"Which children?"

"How many children do we have, for chrissake? It's Jan and Paul. They looked at me like they thought I was crazy."

"Well, at least they got that right. Do you want me to answer the door and let them in?"

"No . . . I want you to leave . . . no . . . go hide in the bedroom."

"Take it easy, sweetheart. Just tell them you're busy and they can come back later."

"Okay." He walked quickly toward her bedroom and closed the door, and with shaking hands, Amanda put the chain on, and pulled open the front door two inches to talk to her daughter. "Hi." She smiled brightly at them from behind the door. "Happy New Year."

"Mom, are you okay?"

"No, actually . . . yes . . . I'm fine. I'm busy . . . I have a headache . . . I'm hungover. Well, actually, I'm not. I had two glasses of Champagne last night. I think I'm allergic to it."

"Mom, why were you naked on the doorstep? The neighbors might see you."

"No one saw me."

"We did."

"I'm sorry. Well, thank you for coming by, sweetheart. Why don't you both come back later. Like tonight maybe. Or tomorrow. That would be perfect." Her words were flying like bullets.

"Why can't we come in now?" Jan was looking extremely worried, but Paul didn't want to push it. It was obviously a bad time. They tried to call first instead of just dropping by, but she hadn't answered the phone. He didn't even think she would be there.

"You can't come in now because of my . . . my headache . . . I'm sleeping."

"You're not sleeping. You came out to pick up the paper. Mom, what's going on?"

"Nothing. I love you, call me next time you want to drop by. That's only polite, sweetheart . . . it's rude to just drop by . . . but I'm glad you did . . . I'll talk to you later. . . ." She gave a little wave, and slammed the door on them. They stood on the doorstep for a minute and then turned and walked back to their car, looking puzzled. It was only when they got back in the car again that Jan looked at her husband with eyes filled with worry.

"Do you think my mother has a drinking problem?"

"Of course not. She just didn't want visitors at this hour. She has a right to that. Hell, maybe she's having an affair with someone, and the guy was still inside. She's still young enough to do stuff like that, you know . . . and your dad's been gone a year. . . ." He looked amused by his own suggestion and Jan looked at him with outrage.

"Are you nuts? *My mother?* Do you actually think she would do that? Don't be ridiculous, just because your father never gets out of bed, at his age, doesn't mean my mother is going to behave that way. Paul, that's disgusting."

"Stranger things have happened." They were halfway through Bel Air by then, and Amanda was back in her bedroom. Jack had just turned on the shower, and he was grinning at her when she closed the bedroom door and leaned against it, as though fleeing from Interpol in a foreign country.

"What did you tell them? Did you tell them I said hi?" He was amused by her reaction.

"That is the most embarrassing thing that's ever happened to me in my entire life. My children will never forgive me."

"What, for not letting them in? They should have called first."

"They did. We didn't answer."

"Then they shouldn't have come by. Simple lesson. Do you want to take a shower?"

"No, I want to die." She threw herself on her bed, and he sat down on the edge of it, and looked at her with deep affection.

"You put yourself through an awful lot of shit. Do you know that?"

"I deserve it," she said, with tears in her eyes again. "I'm a terrible person, and one day my children will know it." And then she looked up at Jack with utter panic as she lay there. "You won't tell

Paul, will you? Oh my God . . . he'll tell Jan, and she'll tell Louise. . . ."

"And the next thing you know, it'll be all over the papers. Hell, sweetheart, Paul and I always talk about the women I sleep with. You cannot take that away from me now. He'll think I'm too old to get it up. . . ."

"Oh my God. Just kill me." She rolled over on her stomach and put her face in the pillow while he grinned at her, and leaned over to kiss her spine in little tiny bits and inches. He kissed her all the way from the top of her neck to her bottom. And then he rubbed her back for a minute, and she rolled over slowly, with eyes that reminded him of the night before, and its effect on him was impressive, and instant. She reached her arms up to him, without saying anything, and he leaned down and kissed her, wanting her more than ever.

"I love you, you crazy thing. . . ." It had been quite a morning.

"I love you too," she whispered hoarsely, and pulled him toward her, but this time he looked down at her with a question.

"Wait a minute, before you walk me into this windmill again, would you like to go to another room, or get off the bed maybe . . . how about the couch or the bathtub?" he asked, as he gently felt her breasts, and then let his hands wander slowly downward.

"Never mind . . . it's okay. . . ." She was smiling at him, and he laughed softly.

"You say that now . . . but what about later?" he whispered.

"You may have to make love to me again, just to calm me down. . . . I think it has a soothing effect . . . it's very therapeutic . . ." she said, reaching out for him, and touching him with her lips until he moaned softly. "I love you, Jack," she said as she touched him again gently.

"I love you too, baby," he said, and then their passion took over, and the insanity of the morning was instantly forgotten.

Chapter Seven

The rest of the New Year weekend went peacefully. Jan called her mother to check on her once, but Amanda was careful to reassure her. She called Louise too, and Jack called Julie, and then Jan and Paul to wish them a Happy New Year.

They stayed at Amanda's house on New Year's Day, made love again that afternoon, and that night went to Malibu to stay at his place. He had a small, comfortable house he had lived in for years, filled with well-loved, handsomely worn objects. There were deep leather chairs, tables covered with books, and some beautiful artwork. And she was surprised to find how at home she felt there.

They walked on the beach the next day, holding hands, and talked about their children. She was still worried about Jan, and hoped that she would be able to get pregnant.

"It's going to kill her if she doesn't," Amanda said sadly. Having children had meant a lot to her, and she could easily imagine how traumatic it would be for Jan not to have them.

"What about you?" Jack asked her quietly on the way back to the house that afternoon.

"What about me?" She didn't understand the question.

"I don't want you to get pregnant," he said honestly. "I assume that's still an issue." At fifty she was still on the cusp, but she was still so youthful in so many ways, he didn't think her body had changed yet. They had been careful anyway, and he was always responsible about the risk of AIDS, particularly given his previously somewhat libertine lifestyle. But he had been inactive for a while, mostly due to coincidence and circumstance, and the enormous demands of the Christmas season at Julie's. And ever since Amanda had crossed his path, he had had no interest in other women. But after his next AIDS test in the upcoming few days, he would like to give up condoms. But the last thing he wanted was to get her pregnant.

"I never thought of that," she said, glancing up at him. She had been faithful to her husband for twenty-seven years, including the past year since he died. "I can't imagine that at my age that's really a problem." She hadn't gotten pregnant in over twenty years, not since a miscarriage she'd had when Jan was in kindergarten. She still remembered how disappointed she'd been, and how traumatic it was. But the thought of getting pregnant now seemed just plain silly, and she said so.

"Not half so silly as the sight of me running away to Brazil, or signing up as a merchant seaman," he said bluntly, and she laughed, but he didn't. He'd been through that often enough over the years, women who claimed they were pregnant by him, or called to say they were late, or had forgotten to take the pill. It was a constant headache.

"Well, wait a while," she smiled. "One of these days, I guess it won't be a problem." She had thought about the change, but had no sign of it yet. Her doctor had said it might not happen for another year or two, or more. And unlike Jan, she had never had a problem getting pregnant.

"I can hardly wait," he grinned, but he also agreed with her. Even if technically she still could get pregnant, at fifty it didn't seem very likely.

He cooked dinner for her that night, and they sat in front of the fire and watched the full moon hang over the ocean. It was easier for her here, she didn't have to think of Matt. Suddenly, it seemed like a whole new life with Jack Watson. It was amazing to her how, after the agony of the past year, and feeling as though her life had ended, she suddenly felt new again, and young and alive, and as though they had been meant for each other. She wondered if it was wrong to move on this way, but she knew that even if it was, she could no longer stop it. All she wanted was to be with him.

They felt like orphans when he went back to work. She didn't know what to do with herself, and he called her half a dozen times a day, and came by the house for lunch, to make love to her, or just to be with her. And when he went back to the store, she always thought of a multitude of reasons to call him, or to ask him something.

"Am I being a pest?" she asked one day. It was the second time she had called him in an hour. And he had only left her half an hour before that. They were going to their favorite Thai restaurant that evening. It was the perfect hideaway, and they knew they wouldn't run into anyone they knew there. She still didn't want to bump into their children. For the time being anyway, they had agreed to keep the romance a secret.

"You're never a pest. I love talking to you," he smiled, putting his feet on his desk, as Gladdie came in with a cup of coffee and he thanked her. And then he had an idea. "Why don't we go to San Francisco for the weekend? I have another site I want to look at up there, on Post Street."

"I'd love that," she said. They decided to go that week, and after he hung up, Jack buzzed for Gladdie. She came in with a worried frown, and her notepad.

"Something wrong?" He looked up at her. In the

past six months, they'd had six shipments held up in customs.

"I probably shouldn't ask," she said with obvious concern, "but are the kids okay?"

"Sure. Why?" He seemed surprised. Maybe she knew something he didn't.

"I've just noticed that Mrs. Kingston has been calling you. I thought maybe . . . I wondered if Paul and Jan . . ." She was embarrassed to ask him. But they'd been married for three years, had no kids, and the world moved pretty fast in L.A. Maybe they were having problems, and Amanda and Jack were talking about them.

"No, they're fine," he said cryptically with a smile, and as their eyes met, Gladdie suddenly wondered. No one else had been calling him since Christmas. No one important anyway, and even when they did call, he had Gladdie tell "the girls" he was busy. It took her a minute, but sharp Gladdie got the picture.

"I see," she said, suddenly amused. Amanda was quite something. But Gladdie would never have thought . . . life sure was funny.

"Just make sure no one else sees, Glad. We don't want the kids to know yet."

"Is it serious?" She was so close to him, and had worked for him for so long, that she dared to ask him questions no one else would. She was privy to a lot of information.

He hesitated for a beat before he answered.

"Could be . . ." And then he decided to be honest with her. He was crazy about Amanda. He had never felt like this for any woman since Dori, and Gladdie never knew her. All she knew were the collection of beautiful women who had filed through his life since she'd been there. "Yes, it is." Their eyes met as he nodded, and he looked happier and younger than she had ever seen him.

"Wow! That's pretty impressive. The kids'll be pleased, won't they?"

"I think so, but Amanda doesn't. We're going to wait a while to see how it goes before we tell them." He asked her to make reservations for them then, in the presidential suite at the Fairmont, and an appointment with the realtor for the space on Post Street.

They flew up to San Francisco on Friday afternoon, and as she walked through the fabulous suite with the unforgettable view, it felt like a honeymoon to Amanda. They had dinner at Fleur de Lys the first night, and room service on the second. And on Saturday they went to look at the commercial space, and he got excited about it in spite of himself. Despite the inevitable headaches of opening a new store, he was falling in love with the idea of bringing Julie's to San Francisco, and he said as much to Amanda.

"I must be nuts to even contemplate the headaches that go with it, at my age." But lately he had been feeling about half his age, ever since he'd been with Amanda. And he couldn't stop talking about ideas for the new store, the architecture, the decor, the subtly different merchandise he wanted to sell here. He felt like a kid again, and he had always had a soft spot for San Francisco.

He wouldn't really mind spending some time there, particularly if Amanda joined him. They talked about it as they walked back to the hotel from Union Square. It was a steep walk up the hill, and they were breathless but exhilarated when they got back to the Fairmont. He was in great spirits, and so was she, especially when they went back to bed for the rest of the morning.

She hated to leave on Sunday afternoon. It had been the perfect weekend, and on Monday she had lunch with her daughters at the Bistro. Louise was looking well, but Jan seemed very down, and Amanda was worried that she had had bad news from her doctor. But before she could ask her daughters anything, they both commented on how well she looked.

"You look terrific, Mom," Jan said, looking relieved. She had been worried about her again ever since New Year's. Maybe it had just been a bad morning, but her mother's behavior had been so odd.

"Thank you, sweetheart. So do you." But Jan's eyes looked so sad. They were halfway through lunch before she decided to talk about it.

"Well, Paul finally went to the doctor," she said,

after a pause, and then tears filled her eyes as she continued. Amanda reached out and touched her hand, and for once even Louise looked worried about her.

"And?" her sister prompted her. "Is he sterile?"

"No," she said, wiping away a tear, "he's fine. And so am I. They have no idea why we haven't gotten pregnant. They just said it might take more time, or maybe it'll never happen. They said that even perfectly healthy people don't get pregnant sometimes. No one knows why. I guess it's just not meant to happen." She started to cry and Amanda reached into her handbag for a tissue. Jan blew her nose and then sighed and went on. "Maybe we'll just never have kids. I asked Paul about adoption again, and he said he'd rather not have children. He only wants a baby that's part of his biological family, so that rules out any kind of adoption." She looked devastated and Amanda's heart felt as though it were breaking.

"He might change his mind, sweetheart. And you might still get pregnant. I'm sure you will. Sometimes it takes people a very long time. And then you'll probably have four in a row and wish you could stop it." They both tried to cheer her up, but it was obvious from the way she looked at them that Jan didn't believe them. And when Amanda told Jack about it that night, he was sorry for both of them.

"Poor kids. Christ, and when I think of all the times I've teased him. He must be ready to kill me."

"I don't know if he's as upset about it as she is," Amanda said pensively, she was deeply worried about her daughter. She had looked so down about it, and so hopeless.

"Maybe if they forget about it for a while, it will just happen."

"That's what I told her. But I think in circumstances like this, it's all you think about. I have friends who went through it." He nodded, and they talked of other things. They always seemed to have a thousand things to say to each other. He talked to her a lot about the store, and asked her opinion about lines he was buying, particularly the high-end ones. She had great taste and a good eye, and she had already made some useful suggestions. And now he was particularly interested in her input in the store he was planning to open in San Francisco. The opening probably wouldn't be for another year or more, but he wanted to get started.

She liked going to the store on Rodeo to visit him, and Gladdie was impressed each time she saw her. There was no question that Amanda was very striking, but she was also very human, and the two women chatted sometimes. Gladdie was their only confidante and she loved knowing their secret.

The entire month flew by. They spent a weekend in Palm Springs, and in February he took her skiing in Aspen. They had a fabulous time, and ran into a number of his friends, all of whom recognized her. They were enormously impressed to see him with her, and much to her chagrin, there was a small blurb about them in the Aspen paper.

"I hope no one calls L.A. This is no way to tell the children."

"Maybe we ought to tell them ourselves one of these days." They had been inseparable for nearly two months now. And they'd been careful to avoid the L.A. press, by staying away from the kind of events that they covered.

But when she had lunch with Jan and Louise again, Jan was still so depressed that Amanda didn't have the heart to tell them. It seemed selfish somehow to brag about her own happiness when Jan was so unhappy. The only time she smiled was when she laughed and said something about Paul's father.

"Paul thinks he has a serious girlfriend. He's really settled down. Paul says he looks half his age, and goes around grinning like a Cheshire cat. But he doesn't say anything about her. She's probably some nineteen-year-old bimbo. But whoever she is, she seems to be keeping him happy and out of trouble."

"Knowing him," Louise said with a look of disdain, "it's probably a set of quintuplets."

"Now, girls, poor man . . . he has a right to his own life," Amanda said nervously, feeling awkward.

"When did you get so charitable about him?" Louise asked, and then the conversation turned to other things. Amanda felt as though she had swallowed her napkin as she looked at them, wondering how she was ever going to tell them.

Amanda told Jack about it that night, and he laughed at her. "You act like you expect them to think you're a virgin."

"Worse. I'm their mother. You know what that means. No sex, no boys, no hanky-panky, except with their father."

"They're adults. They can take it."

"Maybe." But he hadn't convinced her. She knew her daughters.

They were staying in Malibu a lot these days, the weather was warm, the beach was heavenly, and she loved being in his house with him. Even after the initial shock of sleeping with him, she was still a little uncomfortable in her own house. It was easier staying at Jack's place. And she cooked breakfast for him every morning, before he left for work and she went back to her own place.

She was scrambling eggs for him the week before Valentine's Day when he wandered into the kitchen, and was surprised to see her looking unhappy.

"Something wrong?" She was always so sunny in the morning that it surprised him. He had the paper under one arm, and he stopped to kiss her on his way to get coffee.

"I don't know . . . not really . . . I don't feel well." She'd had a headache the day before, and she was feeling slightly queasy. But lately, after thinking it would never happen to her, she had begun to think her body was going through changes. The signs had been very slight, but nonetheless she had noticed and wondered about it. "Louise's kids had the flu last week when I dropped by. I probably caught it from them." She glanced over her shoulder and smiled at him. "It's not terminal. I'll survive it."

"I hope so," he said, looking happy and relaxed as he handed her a mug of coffee. She set it down, and finished his eggs and toast. She had made a big bowl of fruit for him, and she nibbled on a piece of dry toast as she sat down at the table with him, with her coffee. She took a sip, and suddenly just the smell of it overwhelmed her, and he saw it. "You okay?"

"I'm fine. But I think there's something wrong with the coffee. Has it been here for a while?"

He shook his head, and then picked up the paper. "I just bought it. Same brand I always buy. I thought you liked it." He looked disappointed. He liked pleasing her and doing whatever he could to make her happy.

"I do like it usually. It must be me. I'll be fine in a minute." But after he left for work, she lay down, and she still felt queasy when she drove home later that morning. He called her there and offered to meet her for lunch somewhere, but she told him she thought she should try to sleep off her headache. And by that evening, when he picked her up, she was feeling better. And the next day she was fine. It obviously had been the flu. The next morning even the coffee tasted fine, and she was her usual bright self. Until Valentine's Day, when he brought her a five-pound box of chocolate.

"Good lord! I'm going to weigh four hundred pounds if I eat this."

"Good. You need it." He had sent her two dozen long-stemmed red roses that morning, and he was taking her to L'Orangerie for dinner, and he said he didn't give a damn if their children saw them. He opened the box of chocolates for her, and she picked one of the ones she liked best, but the moment she put it in her mouth, she couldn't eat it. He saw the look on her face, and raised an eyebrow. "Are you feeling sick again?" She'd been fine all week, but just as the coffee had the week before, the chocolate made her feel queasy.

"I'm fine," she reassured him, and forced herself to eat the chocolate. But when he ordered caviar for her at L'Orangerie, she got that look again, and no matter how hard she tried, she just couldn't swallow it, although she usually loved it.

"I think you should go to a doctor." He looked worried. She was normally so healthy, and so exuberant, that her obviously feeling so ill frightened him more than he wanted to tell her.

"Louise's kids had this thing for three weeks. Honestly, it's nothing." But she looked green, and she scarcely touched her dinner.

But in spite of his concerns about her, it was a nice evening anyway. They were both in good spirits, and that night they stayed at her place. They made love when they got home, and it was the happiest Valentine's Day she could remember.

And the next morning, sitting in her kitchen, she finally agreed to tell their children.

"Why not share our happiness with them?" he asked. What they had together was such a wondrous thing that he wanted them to know about it.

"Maybe you're right," she agreed. "They're old enough to deal with it."

"They better be. We're grandparents, and if they can't deal with knowing about us, they deserve a spanking."

That afternoon, Jack called Julie, and Amanda called Louise and Jan and they invited them all to dinner at Amanda's. She was going to cook dinner for them, and then afterward, over Champagne, they would tell them. And at least then, as Jack pointed out, they could come out of hiding and go anywhere they wanted. They just wanted them to know that they were happy and in love. There had never been any talk of marriage between them, and Amanda knew full well how strongly Jack felt against it. His first wife had completely cured him.

They set the date for the next week, which, miraculously, suited everyone. Jack said he'd bring the Champagne, and Amanda was busy planning the dinner. There was something very touching about it, and very poignant. And she couldn't help thinking about Matt that afternoon, and how her life had changed. She had loved him deeply for so many years, but he was gone, and she wasn't. Her life had moved on. And hard as it was to believe after so long, she was very much in love with Jack Watson.

She worked frantically all week organizing the dinner and by the time the day came she was a nervous wreck. But when Jack arrived with the wine, the table was set, dinner was well on its way, and she looked lovely.

"I hate to say it, but you don't look like anyone's mother. Certainly not a bunch of kids the age of ours."

"Thank you," she smiled, and kissed him, and she could feel his desire for her as he held her. She laughed as he looked at his watch and then at her, and she shook her head. "We don't have time, you monster."

"Well, if you open the door naked again, we won't have to tell them anything. Look at it that way."

"Later," she promised, and kissed him again. Just touching her drove him crazy.

Julie and Louise and their husbands arrived on time, and Jan and Paul came shortly after. Everyone looked nice, and they all commented on how pretty the house looked. Amanda had put flowers everywhere, and there seemed to be an aura of celebration. But both Jan and Louise looked enormously surprised to see Jack there. He came out of the kitchen, opening a bottle of wine, and greeted everyone with ease, and then kissed Jan, and his daughter. Julie had already figured it out by then. She had been wondering all week why he had invited her to come to dinner at Amanda's, and she had been very suspicious. After that, it wasn't hard to deduce, for her at least, what he was going to tell them. All she wanted to know was if they were getting married, but she decided to wait and see what they told them.

Jan was very cool to him, and Louise was downright rude, and openly ignored him. And everyone except Julie looked worried. She had a live-and-let-live attitude about everything that had always made everyone love her. She had a happy marriage, good kids, and she had always loved her father, in spite of his outrageous behavior. Paul had always been far more critical of him, and Julie had always suspected he was jealous. Paul was so much milder, more afraid, and although he was handsome, he had never had their father's startling good looks. And as he sat down in Amanda's living room, Paul already looked angry, and he and his wife were exchanging suspicious glances.

The conversation at dinner was strained, although the dinner was good, and it was obvious that Amanda had gone to a lot of trouble. And Jack did his best to help her, he talked easily with everyone, and tried to draw them out in conversation, but it was like trying to drag a grand piano. And finally at dessert, he poured the Champagne, looked around the room, and said that there was something he and Amanda wanted to tell them.

"Oh God, I can't believe this," Louise said loudly.

"Why don't you wait until we tell you?" Jack said

pleasantly, and she looked daggers at him. She had never liked him. And neither had Amanda—she would have liked to remind her of it at that moment.

"Your mother and I," he glanced at Jan and Louise, and then at his own son and daughter, "Amanda and I have been seeing each other for a while. We enjoy each other's company a great deal, and we're very happy together, and we wanted you to know it. That's all, nothing more than that, but we thought you should know what we were up to, and we were both sure," he smiled at the woman who had brought him so much happiness in the last two and a half months, "that you would all be happy for us."

"Well, don't be," Louise said tartly, and Amanda looked both crushed and startled. "This is ridiculous. You brought us here to tell us that? That you're sleeping with each other, and we're supposed to congratulate you for it? That's disgusting."

"So is your attitude, Louise," Amanda said firmly. "That's an extremely rude thing to say." She glanced apologetically at Jack, and then back at her daughter.

"This is an extremely rude thing to do," Louise said, with open fury, "to bring us here, to my father's house, to tell us that you two are having an affair. My God, don't you have any decency left, Mom? What about Daddy?"

"What about Daddy?" Amanda said, looking right at her daughter. "I loved your father very much, and you know it. But Daddy's gone, Louise. It was a terrible shock for all of us, me more than anyone.

There were times last year when I thought I wouldn't survive it, when I even wanted to kill myself because I didn't want to live without him. But I have a right to live my life again, and Jack has been wonderful to me." She reached out and touched his hand, and glanced at him. He was looking upset and worried. "He's a kind, decent man, and he makes me very happy, Louise."

"Why don't you just tell us about your sex life, Mom? And how long has this been going on? Did it start before Daddy died? Were you having an affair with him then? Is that it?"

"Louise! How dare you say that! You know that's not true. I started seeing Jack after Jan took me to a party at Julie's."

"Oh my God . . . I can't believe this. . . ." Jan looked at her mother and started to cry, and Paul was shooting dark, angry looks at his father. Jerry, Louise's husband, was staring at his dinner plate, and wishing he didn't have to be there. This was not his problem.

"Why don't you all just calm down for a minute, and let's all act like grown-ups, why don't we?" Julie's was the voice of reason, and Amanda was suddenly grateful to her, although she scarcely knew her.

"I think that's a good idea," Jack said in the brief breach when everyone was marshaling their forces. "Let's have some Champagne." He poured for everyone, and the entire room sat in stony silence. He picked up his glass, and held it up to Amanda. "To you, sweetheart, thank you for a beautiful dinner." There were tears in her eyes, and no one touched their glasses.

"So when are you two getting married?" Louise was looking at them with revulsion and open fury.

"We're not." Jack spoke for them. "There's no reason to. We're not your age. We're not going to have kids. We can have a good life together without making it legal." Julie smiled, she knew him well, and how much he hated even the idea of marriage. "No one's going to lose any money on this deal, if that's what you're all worried about." He was more than a little annoyed at them, and Amanda could hear it. "No one is going to lose anything. But what you've gained is two happy parents. We love you, and we wanted to share our happiness with you. It doesn't seem like a lot to ask, to ask you all to be happy for us, and gracious about it." He was furious at their collective reaction.

"How could you do this, Mom?" Jan asked with tears streaming down her cheeks. "You *hate* him!" she said, looking daggers at Jack, and he laughed and took Amanda's hand in his own.

"I don't think so, Jan. And we care a lot about your happiness and Paul's. We talk about you all the time . . . that's why it was important to us to tell you."

"Well, I think you're both disgusting and pathetic," Louise said, standing up from the table.

"You would think that people your age could keep your pants on, for chrissake. My father's hardly been dead a year, and I guess Little Old Hot Pants Mom just couldn't wait to get out and party."

"Louise!" Amanda stood up with a look of fury. "Do you remember how depressed I was, and how worried you all were about me?"

"Little did we know what you'd do when you recovered. Well," she said derisively, with a pointed look at her husband, which brought him to his feet beside her, "it was certainly a great evening, and I hope you two little rabbits will be very happy." With that, she strode to the door, picked up her jacket on the way out, and slammed the door behind them, as Jan burst into tears again and Paul held her.

"Jan, please," Amanda said, with a look of sorrow. It had been a terrible evening for all of them, but mostly for Jack, and for her.

"Mom, how could you do this? Why did you tell us? Don't you know how embarrassing this is for us? We don't want to know about it."

"Why not?" Jack asked without embarrassment. "Why shouldn't your mother share her life with you? Don't you want her to be happy?" He sounded so reasonable that Jan looked at him and stopped crying.

"Why can't she be happy alone? Why can't she just remember my father?"

"Because she's a young, vital, beautiful woman,

Jan. Why should she be alone? Is that what you would do if something happened to Paul?"

"That's different."

"Why? Because you're younger than we are? Even people our age have a right not to be alone, to companionship, to happiness, to love. . . ."

"This isn't about 'love,'" Paul said darkly. "We all know that about you, Dad, don't we?"

"Maybe you don't know me as well as you think you do, Son."

"I'm happy for you, Dad," Julie said quietly, and came around the table to kiss him, and then she went and did the same to Amanda, and there were tears in Amanda's eyes as she thanked her. She was the only one who had been decent to them. The others had been a nightmare.

"I'm sorry this has been so hard for all of you," Amanda said quietly, dabbing at her eyes with her napkin. She felt as though she were going to start sobbing any minute, and she didn't want to give them that satisfaction, but it was incredibly hard not to. "We didn't want to upset you, but it seemed more honest to tell you. I didn't want to lie to you." She looked at Jan, and in the same instant Jan realized that Paul had been right on New Year's Day with his outrageous suggestion. There had been a man in the house. It was Paul's father. She closed her eyes in horror.

"We hope you'll adjust in time," Jack said quietly, and Paul said something in a whisper to Jan, and they both got up and left the table, and put their coats on.

"We're going," Jan said, looking like an angry child from the doorway. It was exactly the way she had looked when she was five years old and getting ready to have a tantrum.

"I love you," Amanda said sadly from the table, too beaten to get up, or try to stop her. And the door closed softly behind them, as Julie and her husband stood up, and she came around again to her father. She was a pretty girl and she looked just like him.

"I'm sorry, Dad. They were awful."

"They sure were." He glanced at Amanda with a worried expression. She had predicted that it would be hard for them, but neither of them had expected this onslaught.

"They'll get over it. I think part of it is just the shock of knowing that their dad has been replaced in some ways," and then she smiled, "and it's hard to think of your parents having fun . . . and having sex." She blushed. "You guys are supposed to be institutions, not people," she said wisely, and her father smiled proudly at her. She was a terrific young woman, and in their own way, so were the others, but they didn't have the largeness of spirit that she did.

"I guess it was too much for them. You were right," he glanced at Amanda, "we shouldn't have told them."

"I'm glad we did," she said, and totally surprised

him. She left her place at the table and came to stand next to him, with Julie and her husband. "We did the right thing, and if they can't live with it or even try to deal with it, then that's not our problem. We have a right to more in our lives than just being parents. The only thing that bothers me is that I never realized I had such totally selfish children. But I'm not giving up my life for them. I'm not going to stop being there for them, or loving them, and if they can't be there for me, then that's their loss." Julie put her arms around her then, and Amanda's chin quivered as she held her. And a few minutes later, Julie and her husband left, and Jack took Amanda in his arms and she sobbed piteously. And he felt desperately sorry for her. The evening had been such a disappointment.

"I'm so sorry, sweetheart. What a bunch of rotten kids we have," he said, with a smile. But he was angry that they had hurt her.

"Yours are fine, or Julie at least. Mine were the ones who were awful."

"They want their daddy. And they don't think you have a right to a life with anyone else. It's pretty simple. I didn't take it personally. I understand it. But I hate what they did to you. They'll get over it."

"Maybe." She didn't sound convinced, but oddly enough it didn't make her regret anything they had done. It only made her feel closer to Jack, and that night they went to Malibu, after she cleaned up the dining room and put the dishes in the dishwasher.

She didn't want to be in the house where her children had been so unpleasant to them. She wanted to be at Jack's, in his big comfortable bed, in his arms, and she wanted to forget everything that had happened.

She still looked sad when they went to bed that night, and he held her in his arms, and they talked about it for a long time. He wished that there was some way he could make it better.

"Give them time, sweetheart. I guess even at their age, it's a big adjustment."

"They're happy. Why can't I be?"

"Because you're their mom. You heard what Julie said. Parents, and certainly people our age, aren't supposed to have sex, God forbid. They think it's disgusting."

"They should only know . . . it's a lot better than it was at their age."

"Shhh . . . let's keep that a secret!" he said, and kissed her tenderly, and a moment later she could feel how aroused he was and how much he wanted her, and she wanted him just as badly. They made love hungrily, and afterward, he heard a soft chuckle in the darkness. "What are you laughing at?" But he was pleased that she was obviously feeling better.

"That morning on New Year's Day when Jan saw me naked on the doorstep, and I wouldn't let her in. She must be having a fit over it. I guess I looked pretty silly."

"You looked pretty good to me . . . 'silly' isn't a

word I would have used to describe you." But she had been silly that day, and they both knew it. She had been in a total panic.

"Maybe we should put the children up for adoption," she said sleepily, turning on her side toward him, as he kissed her.

"That's a great idea. We'll invite them to dinner and tell them."

"Hmmm . . . great idea . . . you bring . . . the . . . Champagne. . . ." But she was already asleep in his arms as she said it, and he looked at her with a slow smile. She was quite a woman, and he wouldn't have given her up for anything in the world, no matter what their kids said, or how angry they were at them. He was going to hang on to her now for dear life.

Chapter Eight

The rest of February disappeared in the blink of an eye, and in March the children were still cool to Amanda. She and Jack talked about it from time to time, and he knew how much it bothered her, but there was nothing they could do about it, except wait for them to come around once they'd adjusted. Jan hardly ever called her mother anymore, and Louise was openly hostile to her whenever Amanda went to visit the children. In her case, her reaction was particularly hard to understand, since she had never gotten along with her father.

But Amanda and Jack were so busy these days that at least most of the time, she was distracted. But there was no denying that her daughters' reaction to them was taking a toll on her. She seemed to have stomach problems all the time, and constant indigestion. And Jack was still urging her to go to see a doctor.

"This has gone on for a while. I think you should check it out. You could be getting an ulcer."

"I could be." She hadn't been able to drink coffee in weeks, and she had been exhausted ever since the unhappy meeting with her children, but she also knew that it was very obviously due to her own emotions. She had hated to see them all so angry. And once in a while now, she had nightmares about Matthew. He always accused her of something in her dreams, and any psychiatrist probably would have told her she felt guilty. But not enough so to change her feelings. She was more in love with Jack than ever. And the romance had blossomed.

He invited her to the Academy Awards in March. They were early this year, and he was always invited by his more important clients. Amanda hadn't been to them in years, not since she won one herself, and she was excited about going with him. And he ordered a dress for her from Julie's. It was a fabulous white satin Jean-Louis Scherrer with black-beaded shoulders and a small train that lingered elegantly behind her. And when the big night came, and he picked her up, she took his breath away. She looked every inch a queen, and the big star she had once been. It was as though, with him, she had regained what she had once been, and added to it. In the past few months, she had acquired a patina of happiness over her old glamour.

"Wow!" he said admiringly. The dress hadn't looked half as beautiful when he first saw it. On her, it looked exquisite, and it molded every inch of her fabulous figure. Her long blond hair was piled high on her head in soft curls and a French twist. And she was wearing diamond earrings and a diamond bracelet. She looked truly splendid.

"You look incredible!" he said with a low whistle. Her skin was as creamy pale as the white satin. "The photographers are going to go crazy."

"I doubt that," she said modestly, and took his arm as they walked out to the waiting limousine. He was carrying her short white mink jacket.

When they stepped out of the car at the Shrine Auditorium, the crowd cheered for her. They recognized her immediately, and shouted her name, and just as he had predicted, a wall of photographers engulfed them. He could feel her hand shake a little as he took it in his own and he smiled down at her. Her husband had kept her away from all this for more than twenty years, and now suddenly she was back, and no longer accustomed to it. There was an elegant, gentle grace about her that made her even more alluring.

"Are you all right?" he asked, looking at her with concern. She looked a little nervous, but she smiled up at him and nodded.

They made their way through the press, and the

crowds in the lobby, and then slowly to their seats in the auditorium, among all the stars that the entire country and world adored and longed for. Several people waved at them, and Jack smiled broadly at a number of his clients. He looked proud and at ease, and completely comfortable to be there.

And then the ceremony began, and as usual, it took forever. The TV cameras panned across them constantly, and they all felt as though they'd been there all year by the time it was over. The award for Best Actor had gone to a new face this year, and the Oscar for Best Actress had gone to an old favorite who had held her prize aloft and gave a whoop of glee while everyone got to their feet and cheered her.

"Finally!" she said with a huge smile. It had taken her forty years to win it. And Amanda couldn't help remembering how she had felt nearly thirty years before on a night like this. It had been one of the most exciting things that had ever happened to her. And now, it seemed so long ago, and still a warm memory, but so much less important.

"What was it like for you?" he asked with a smile, as they left the auditorium through throngs that barely seemed to move. It was worse than riding the New York subway.

"It was incredible," she said, smiling at him. "I thought I was going to explode with excitement. I never even thought I'd get the nomination, let alone win it. I was twenty-two . . . it was terrific." It was nice to be able to admit how much it had meant to her. Her husband had never liked it when she talked about it.

They barely moved ten feet in the next ten minutes, and people kept coming up to them, to talk and comment on the awards and just to say hello, as they all waited to leave the theater. The press was complicating everything, stopping stars as they left, and interviewing them right in the midst of the crowd, creating bottlenecks that couldn't be passed through.

"Think we'll ever get out of here tonight?" Jack Nicholson asked as they pressed by him, and Amanda shook her head with a smile. She had never met him, but admired him greatly.

"Do you know him?" Jack asked with interest.

"No. But I like his movies."

"We should rent yours sometime," he said. He had never thought of it, she spoke so little about her career. Matthew had taught her not to.

"How depressing," she laughed. "I can't think of anything worse than seeing what I looked like thirty years ago, and then having to look at myself in the mirror. Besides, I wasn't much of an actress."

Jack shook his head at her modesty, and they moved a few inches and then were trapped in total gridlock, and the heat and crowd around them was oppressive. She felt as though she were going to melt, and she could just imagine what Jack felt like in his tuxedo. But in spite of the discomforts people were in good spirits, and everyone was laughing and talking and waving at friends they couldn't get to. But just as Jack saw one of his favorite clients about twenty feet away from them, Amanda began to feel dizzy. Jack was mouthing bits of a conversation and pointing to the exits as he rolled his eyes, and Amanda suddenly heard a buzzing in her ears, and her head started pounding. But Jack hadn't noticed. After a while, she tugged at his sleeve, and when he looked back at her, he was startled to see that she had gone deathly pale in just a few minutes.

"I'm not feeling very well," she whispered to him, "it's so hot in here . . . I'm sorry. . . ."

"Do you want to sit down?" He couldn't blame her. It was giving him a headache too, and the camera lights still focused on them weren't helping, and the heat was very oppressive. It was also impossible to reach the seats again. They were trapped in the aisles, and they would have had to fly to get there. Jack realized that as soon as he'd said it, and he glanced at Amanda's face again. She was suddenly not just pale, she was green, and she was blinking as though she was having trouble seeing. He got a firm grip on her arm, and tried to guide her out of the aisle through the crowd, but it was hopeless.

"Jack . . ." she said weakly, looking at him, and as he looked at her, her eyelids fluttered, her eyes rolled back, and she fainted, and he just managed to catch her as a ripple went through the crowd immediately around her, and a woman gasped as she saw it. Jack was holding Amanda in his arms, and somebody started shouting. People were trying to move for them, everyone was asking what had happened, and Jack was worried sick about her.

"Give us some air, please . . . move back!" A man next to him was shouting, "Call the paramedics!" Suddenly it was hysteria all around them, and Amanda was still lifeless in his arms. He swept her off her feet, and her head rested against his chest, just as two ushers appeared out of nowhere with smelling salts and an ice pack, asking what happened. But at the same moment, Amanda began stirring, and glanced up at Jack, with no idea of what had happened to her.

"You fainted, sweetheart . . . it's the heat . . . just take it easy. . . ." And like the Red Sea parting, the crush of people moved just enough to let him carry her to a row of seats and he set her down gently. And within seconds, a crew of paramedics arrived and looked down at Amanda, as Jack explained that she had fainted.

"How do you feel now?" one of the paramedics asked her.

"Incredibly foolish," Amanda said, smiling weakly at Jack with a look of apology. "I'm really sorry."

"Don't be silly," he said, looking worried. She was still light-headed and he could see it. She didn't look as though she could have stood up and walked out of the theater, but she wanted to try it.

"We'll get a wheelchair," one of the ushers offered, and Amanda looked horrified.

"No, really . . . I'm fine. . . . We'll go when the crowd thins out a little."

But the ushers offered to take her out a back exit instead, and Jack urged them to do that. The paramedics said she was free to go, as long as she felt up to it, but they suggested she see her doctor in the morning, and Jack seconded the motion with a grim expression. He had been telling her that for a month, and she wouldn't listen.

He put a powerful arm around her waist, and half carried her to the exit between the ushers, and a moment later they were out in the air, and she felt better. She took a deep breath and thanked everyone, and apologized profusely for the trouble she'd caused them. She was deeply grateful that they hadn't been spotted by the press. There was no one waiting for them, and Jack left her with the ushers just long enough to find the limo, and then came back and got her into it. Five minutes later, they were driving away, and she was leaning against the backseat with an exhausted expression.

"I'm so sorry," she said for the ten thousandth time. "I don't know what happened."

"That's why you have to see the doctor."

"I think it was just the heat and the crowd. I couldn't breathe all of a sudden," she said, sipping a glass of water he handed her from the bar in the limo. "People always faint at the Academy Awards, Jack. I'm just sorry I did it this year."

"Well, don't do it again!" He leaned over and

kissed her. She still looked beautiful, but very pale. And he was very worried about her. "You scared me to death in there. It's a good thing it was so damn crowded, so you couldn't fall when you fainted. At least you didn't hit your head or anything."

"Thank you, Jack." He took such good care of her, and when they got back to his house, she took off her dress, and he tucked her into bed, and she looked like a teenager with her fancy hairdo and her blond hair and her makeup and diamond earrings still on, and then she giggled. "I can't believe I did that."

"It was very dramatic," he chided, loosening his tie, and smiling at her. "Can I get you anything? Water? Tea?" She puckered her brows as she thought about it and then smiled at him. She was starving.

"How about ice cream?"

"Ice cream?" He looked startled at the question. "You must be feeling better at least. I'll see what we've got. What flavor?"

"Mmm . . . coffee."

"Coming right up." He saluted, and came back with a bowlful two minutes later, and one for him too, and he sat on the bed next to her as they ate it. "Maybe you were just hungry," he said hopefully, but he didn't think so. She'd been looking pale lately, and he'd been trying not to see it. She'd been looking great for a while, and now lately, she looked tired. But he knew she was still upset about her children, and they weren't making it any easier for her. They refused to offer any acknowledgment whatsoever, let alone approval, of her relationship with Jack Watson.

But Jack had decided to take the matter in hand himself the next day. As soon as they got up, he asked her for the number and called her doctor. He told the nurse what had happened the night before, and asked for an appointment that morning for Amanda Kingston.

"And you are?" the nurse asked pointedly. She was new there, and she didn't know Amanda.

"Mr. Watson," he said, writing down the time of the appointment.

"Are you Mrs. Kingston's husband?"

"No . . . I'm her friend. I'll be there with her."

"Fine, Mr. Watson. We'll see you at eleven." The appointment was in Beverly Hills, and after he brought Amanda a cup of tea and told her about it, he decided to go for a walk on the beach by himself. She seemed happy to stay in bed that morning, and he suspected correctly that she did not feel as well as she pretended. But he didn't challenge her about it. They would know more, hopefully, when they went to the doctor.

But as he walked down the beach alone, his thoughts seemed to fly in all directions, and he began to run, as though to escape the terror of what he was thinking. Anything was possible . . . she could have a brain tumor . . . bone cancer . . . something that had grown and spread and metastasized without their even knowing it was there. He could only imagine the worst scenarios and when he finally stopped running and sat down, he realized he was crying. But it was happening to him all over again. He had found the one woman in millions he could love, and something terrible was happening to her. He was terrified she was dying. It was going to be just like Dori, he thought as he sobbed, he was going to lose her, and he couldn't bear it. He put his face down on his knees, and huddled there, crying like a child, and he couldn't even turn to her for comfort. He didn't want to frighten her, but more than anything he didn't want to lose her.

He was gone for nearly an hour, and when he came back she was dressed and waiting, and she looked better than she had earlier, but he was still worried. Nothing was going to reassure him now except the word from the doctor that she wasn't suffering from anything terminal, or malignant. He just couldn't stand it. But he spoke to her with forced cheer, as he put his jacket on and looked at his watch. It was time to leave, in case they ran into traffic.

"All set?" he asked nervously. He didn't know why, but he felt as though he were going to the guillotine. It was as though his life was never going to be the same again, and he was never going to come back here to this house again, in the same easy spirit. He was bracing himself for the worst news he could imagine, because he loved her.

"Sweetheart," she said gently, before they left, looking up at him with eyes that tore his heart out, "I'm all right. I promise. They'll probably just tell us I have an ulcer. I had one years ago, when the girls were small, and these days that's pretty simple to deal with. A couple of pills, and it'll disappear like magic."

"You should have gone weeks ago," he reproached her, as they walked to his Ferrari.

"I was busy," she said primly, and got in beside him. She loved riding in the car with him usually, but this morning on the way into town, his fast turns and sharp moves made her feel sick, but she didn't dare tell him. She knew he would have been even more frantic.

Her doctor was in the medical building at 435 North Bedford, the waiting room was full when they got there, and it seemed to take forever. Jack glanced at magazines, and Amanda just sat there with her eyes closed, waiting. He looked over at her from time to time and he hated her pallor and the obvious look of discomfort. He knew she wasn't in pain, he had asked her that, but she just didn't feel well. And there was no way she could still sell him the story about catching the flu from Louise's kids, that had been more than a month before. This was something far more scary.

A nurse in the doorway finally called her name,

and Jack watched as she went in, and smiled at her encouragingly when she glanced over her shoulder. She was nervous too, but they were trying to put a good face on it for each other. But neither of them were convincing.

And even Amanda had to admit that it was a relief to finally sit there with her doctor. He was kind, and a familiar face, and she had gone to him for nearly twenty years. He had also been Matt's doctor, and he asked her now if she was very lonely. She was embarrassed to tell him about Jack, although he was sitting in the waiting room large as life, so she just nodded, and began telling him her symptoms. She told him about the flu the month before, the occasional queasiness, and her absolute inability to drink coffee or eat chocolate, which she took as a sure sign of an ulcer.

He asked her if she'd seen her gynecologist recently and had a mammogram and a Pap smear, and she admitted that she hadn't. She had been due for both when Matt died so suddenly, and just hadn't bothered since then.

"You should, you know," he scolded her. "At your age, you should have both every year." And she promised that she'd take care of it immediately, and then he asked her if she had any warning signs of menopause, and she explained that lately she was beginning to think that she had some.

He nodded. At fifty-one, that didn't surprise him. "Hot flashes?"

"No, not yet. I'm just tired a lot, and irregular." A number of her friends complained of fatigue all the time, although she'd never had that before. But lately, she was constantly exhausted. At first, she had just thought it was a side effect of her new love life. But in the past few weeks, she didn't think so. She could hardly put one foot in front of the other.

He asked her about a lot of other things, and he was inclined to agree with her. Probably the onset of menopause, and possibly an ulcer.

"I'm going to send you to the hospital for a sonogram," he explained to her. "Let's see what that shows, we can always do a GI series after that if it's indicated, but let's not rush into anything yet. And I want you to see your gynecologist tomorrow. He can give you some hormone replacement therapy that may pick you up almost immediately. It's worth talking to him about." She listened and nodded, as he handed her a slip of paper, and told her where to go at Cedars Sinai. And he told her they'd either give her the results there if the radiologist was there, or he'd call her the next day to tell her if she had an ulcer. "All right?" He smiled at her and stood up, and walked her to the door of his office. And then she went to find Jack, who looked grim as he waited, but he broke into a smile the minute he saw her. He looked like a kid who had lost his mother and finally found her. She had been gone for nearly an hour.

"What did he say?"

"Pretty much what I thought. Some . . . um

. . . changes in my body . . . and maybe an ulcer. I have to go to the hospital for a sonogram now. Do you want me to drop you off at the store on the way? I hate to waste your whole day with this nonsense. He took forever."

"I'm coming with you," Jack said firmly, but he was relieved that nothing worse had turned up, at least not so far.

"Did he think there was anything to worry about?" Jack asked as they got to the car, but she shook her head, looking a little mournful.

"He thought I might need hormones. That's depressing enough. I feel like an old woman."

"Oh sweetheart . . . come on . . . You're a baby." He always made her feel better, and she smiled sheepishly as she slipped into the passenger seat in the Ferrari and he roared down North Bedford to Cedars Sinai.

At the hospital, they had to wait forever again, but they finally called her in, and this time Jack decided to come with her. He didn't like hospitals, and he didn't like them messing with her without some supervision. A technician had already explained to them that there was nothing invasive about the test. They would put gel on her abdomen, and roll a transducer around on it, and an image would appear on a screen to tell them if she had any growths or cysts, or possibly an ulcer. It sounded pretty simple. But he still wanted to be with her.

She undressed in a cubicle, and emerged in a

white gown and her shoes, feeling foolish, and he smiled at her as she lay down. They gave him a stool just behind her head, where he could see the screen too, but all it looked like was a weather map of Atlanta. They applied the gel, and the technician began rolling the transducer, much like a microphone, around on her stomach with a little mild pressure. All it felt was cold, and the whole thing was pretty boring. And then they both saw the technician frown, and concentrate on an area low on her stomach. And the pressure of the transducer felt mildly uncomfortable to Amanda while she did it. The technician said she'd be right back, and went to get someone to look at it with her. This time a young resident came, and he introduced himself to both of them, and then glanced at the sonogram with interest.

"Something wrong?" Amanda asked, trying to feign a calm she didn't feel. She was beginning to panic. It was easy to see that they had seen something that either worried or perplexed them. But the resident was nonchalant when he answered.

"Not at all. We just like to be sure of what we see here. Four eyes are better than two sometimes, but I think we have a pretty clear picture. When was your last period, Mrs. Kingston?"

"Two months ago," she said, in a choked voice. She obviously had something wrong with her ovaries . . . or her uterus . . . it wasn't change of life at all

. . . it was cancer. . . . She couldn't even look at Jack as she said it, but the resident nodded.

"That sounds about right," he said, nodding, and then zoomed in the sonogram screen for a closer view, pressed a button, and a white asterisk appeared on the screen over something that was throbbing. "Right here." He pointed at the asterisk with a finger and smiled at them. "Can you see that?" She nodded, and Jack stared at it blindly. Clearly, that was the root of the problem. "Do you know what that is, Mr. and Mrs. Kingston?" At their age, it was obvious to him that they were married. Why else would they be together?

"A tumor?" she asked hoarsely, as Jack closed his eyes in terror.

"A baby. I'd say you're just about two months pregnant. In fact, if you hold for a minute here, I can computerize your due date."

"My *what?*" She sat bolt upright and knocked the transducer right off her stomach. "I'm *what?*" She turned to look at Jack as she heard a noise just behind her, and she turned around just in time to see him slip right off the stool, where he had been sitting, on his way to the floor. He had fainted. "Oh my God . . . I've killed him . . . somebody help him!" Her bare bottom was sticking out of the gown as she bent over him, and he groaned horribly and touched his head as he stirred, and the resident hit a panic button, and a team of paramedics came running. Jack was awake by then, and Amanda could already feel the bump on the back of his head as she knelt beside him. "Oh God . . . I'm so sorry . . . are you okay? . . ." The resident sent the paramedics away and the technician went to get some ice, as Jack sat up slowly.

"I'm fine. I just tried to commit suicide, that's all. Why did you stop me?"

"I take it this is a surprise to both of you," the resident smiled benignly. "It happens that way sometimes, particularly with late babies."

"*Late?*" Amanda turned to look at him. "I thought the show was over."

"Did you think you were experiencing signs of menopause?" he asked, and she nodded, as Amanda helped Jack onto the table. He lay down and she applied the ice pack that the technician had brought them.

"Do you think he has a concussion?" she asked worriedly, but the doctor shone a light in Jack's eyes, and assured her he didn't.

"You're lucky I didn't have a heart attack," Jack said to Amanda. "How did that happen?" But they both knew. They had given up condoms in January, after the results of his AIDS test. She had been so sure she wouldn't get pregnant. It had never occurred to her that this could happen. "I can't believe this," he groaned again and closed his eyes. He had an unbelievable headache.

"Neither can I," Amanda said softly, staring at the frozen image on the screen that was their baby. And

"October 3" had appeared on the screen, since they last looked at it.

"There's your due date," the resident told them happily, and Jack felt an overwhelming desire to kill him. "We'll send a report to your doctor. Congratulations!" And with that, he strode out of the room to the next patient he had to see and the technician handed them a picture that had been spat out of the machine in the last few seconds.

"That's your baby's first picture." She smiled at them both, and began resetting the machine for the next patient. They needed the room, and Jack got up slowly and looked at Amanda.

"I don't believe it," he said hoarsely. He looked worse than she did. She was suddenly feeling much better knowing that at least she didn't have cancer, or even an ulcer. Just a baby.

"I don't believe it either." She glanced at him in embarrassment. "I'll put my clothes on." She was back in a minute, and they walked slowly out of the room, still carrying the bag of ice chips. Jack looked like the patient. Neither of them said a word until they got to the car, and then he just stood there and stared at her. He felt as though his whole life was passing before him. It had happened to him before, but not like this, not with a woman he cared about so much, and not so totally out of the blue like that. With thirty-year-olds, you knew you were in trouble when you took chances. But at fifty-one? Jesus. "I can't believe I'm pregnant." She was still holding the picture and he saw it.

"Throw that thing away. It scares me." The little thing that had been throbbing had been the baby's heart, and the doctor had told them that the fetus was healthy. But she clung to the picture now and looked at it as she sat in the Ferrari. "Do you want to go somewhere and talk? Or just go home and try to absorb it?" He knew this would be a big step for her, and he was sorry for her. It was a shame it had happened to them. But in the end, maybe it would bring them even closer, at least he hoped so. And he planned to be there for her.

"Do you have to go to the office?"

"Probably. But if you want to go talk about it, I'll call Gladdie. You'd better call your doctor." She nodded as he started the car and called Gladdie from the car phone.

"I don't know what to say," Amanda said softly, looking at him. This was terrifying and amazing. She couldn't even think yet of all the implications.

"It's my fault," he said glumly, "I should have been careful. I was just so happy to be rid of those damn things after all these years, I guess I got carried away . . . and pretty stupid."

"I never thought this could happen," she said, still in shock.

"Yeah, teenage pregnancy in your fifties," he smiled at her then, and leaned over and kissed her. "I love you. I'm just glad you're okay, and it was nothing worse." As far as that went, he was relieved, but he was sorry for her. "At least this we can fix," he said comfortingly as they stopped at a stoplight, and she looked over at him in confusion.

"What does that mean?" Her voice was very small and tight as she asked him.

"Well, you're not going to keep the pregnancy, at our age. That's ridiculous. And besides, neither of us wants more kids. What would we do with a baby?"

"What does everyone else do?"

"They're usually twenty years younger than we are, and they're married." And then as he looked at her face, he pulled over. "Are you telling me you want to keep it?" She didn't answer him, but the look in her eyes filled him with terror. "Are you crazy? I'm sixty years old, and you're fifty-one. We're not married, and your children already hate me. How do you think this little piece of news would go over?" He couldn't believe it. It had never even dawned on him that she might want to have the baby.

"It's our life, not theirs . . . and the baby's, Jack, you're asking me to kill a live human being." Her eyes were filled with pain now.

"Bullshit." He was raising his voice to her for the first time since he'd known her. "I'm asking you to be reasonable, for chrissake, Amanda. You cannot consider keeping this baby."

"I will *not* kill it." She hadn't even thought about

it yet, but suddenly she knew clearly, without a moment's doubt, that she didn't want an abortion.

"It's not a baby. It's a blob. It's a nothing on a TV screen. And it's a threat to our sanity, and our life together. Don't you understand that? We can't do this!" He shouted at her, and she glared at him and said nothing. "*I* can't do it, then. I *won't* do it, and you can't force me! I've been through this before, and I'm not going to be pushed into having a kid at my age. You *have* to have an abortion." He wanted to shake her, but he would never have hurt her, even in his total outrage.

"I don't *have* to do anything, Jack. And I'm not some bimbo trying to force you, or trick you, into marriage. I didn't want this either. But I'm not going to be forced into doing something I don't believe in because you're too chickenshit to deal with a little reality here. I *am* pregnant, and it *is* our baby."

"And you *are* crazy. It must be the hormones. Oh my God, I can't believe this," he said, shoving the car into gear and heading toward Bel Air, to her house. "Look," he said, turning to her as he sped down Rodeo, "you can do whatever you want, Amanda, but *I'm* not having this baby. I'm not doing night feedings, and earaches, and Little League. I'm not going to make a fool of myself going to his college graduation when I'm ninety."

"You'd only be eighty. Eighty-two to be exact. And what's more, you're a coward." And as she said it, she began to cry, and he tried to control himself and reason with her.

"Look, sweetheart . . . I know how you must feel. It's a shock. First we thought there was something terrible wrong with you, and now you're pregnant. You're not thinking clearly. An abortion is a terrible thing. I know that. I understand it. But think what this would do to your life, never mind mine. Do you really want to start all over again? Driving car pool at sixty?"

"You seem to do all right driving at your age. I'm sure I could manage to hold on to my license for the next nine years, if I work at it. And no, this isn't what I'd have chosen. I'm not stupid. But it wasn't my choice, or yours, it was God's. He gave us this incredible gift. We don't have the right to just throw it away. . . ." She was crying again as she looked at him, trying to reach him. But she could see it was hopeless, and she bowed her head and just cried then. "Jack, I can't do it."

"You never told me you were religious," he said sadly, feeling betrayed, and sorry for her, but angry anyway. She had no right to do this to him. Dori never would have.

"I feel very strongly about this," she said, in a small, clear voice as they pulled up in front of her house and he looked at her.

"So do I, Amanda. And nothing you say is going to sway me. I won't be a part of it. I don't want to know anything about it. If you have an abortion, I'll be there for you. I'll hold you. I'll cry with you. I'll love you forever. But I am not going to be forced into having a baby at my age." And he meant it.

"Other men your age do it all the time. Especially here, in L.A. Half the fathers I see in my gynecologist's office with their thirty-year-old wives out to here," she showed him and he almost winced, "are older than you are."

"Then they're senile. I'm very clear about how I feel about this. I'm out of here, Amanda, if you have this baby."

"Good-bye then," she said, looking at him with sudden hatred. "Do whatever the hell you want, it's your life, but this is mine, and my body, and my baby. And you can't have any of it, so to hell with you, Jack Watson. Go back to all your stupid bimbos, and I hope you knock them all up. You deserve it."

"Thanks for playing," he said as she got out of the car, and slammed the door so hard it rattled everything in it. And she never looked back as she ran to her house, unlocked the door, and disappeared inside it.

Five seconds later, she heard the Ferrari roar away, and sat down in the front hall and sobbed. She had lost him. She had lost everything . . . but she wasn't going to give in. She had no choice now. She was going to have the baby. But what in God's name was she going to tell the children?

Chapter Nine

The next three days were a nightmare for both of them. For the first time in years, he even shouted at Gladdie. She didn't know what was wrong with him, but whatever it was, she knew it was Big Time. And the fact that Amanda wasn't calling hadn't gone unnoticed. He didn't even take Julie's or Paul's calls, when they phoned him. He spoke to no one.

And Amanda locked herself in her house and acted as though she had gone back into mourning. Louise came by with the kids, and she wouldn't let them in. She told them she had a migraine, and she looked it. She looked awful.

"What's wrong with Mom?" Louise finally called Jan to ask her if she knew anything, but all Jan knew was that her father-in-law wasn't talking to Paul either. "Maybe they broke up, the sex fiends. Please God, tell me it's true. Hallelujah."

"Oh come on, Lou," Jan chided her older sister, and Louise was startled.

"What, are you on their team now?"

"No, but you know, they are adults, and Daddy's gone. Maybe they have a right to do what they want, as long as they do it discreetly."

"Don't give me that. They're disgusting," Louise said bluntly.

"Whatever happened to all that stuff you said after Daddy died, about Mom having a right to her own life now, and all that? Maybe we don't have a right to interfere, or even to disapprove. What makes us the source of all judgment?"

"Shit, Jan. What did you do? Find religion? She's your mother. She's behaving like a slut. She's having an affair."

"She's single and she's over fifty. She has a right to do whatever she wants. I'm beginning to think we all behaved like jerks when she told us."

"Well, I don't. And I just hope he dumped her."

"Maybe she dumped him."

"Just so someone did it."

But by week's end, Amanda still wasn't talking to anyone, and no one had seen her. And both girls were worried. In truth, she was sitting around and crying all the time, from the emotions, and the shock of losing Jack, and the hormones. She felt as though her life was over, and yet at the same time she was overwhelmed at the prospect of a new life just beginning. But she couldn't imagine a life now without Jack. She hadn't heard a word from him since she'd last seen him, and he hadn't even called her.

He was shouting at every employee who crossed him and working till midnight every night. And when he got home, he just sat on the couch, staring into space, trying not to think of her and how she'd betrayed him. He still couldn't believe it. How could she do this to him? It wasn't her fault she'd gotten pregnant, not entirely, but the fact that she wouldn't get rid of it seemed like the ultimate betrayal. And then, just as he'd be thinking how angry he was at her, he would suddenly remember something she had said, or done . . . or the way she looked when he made love to her, or in the morning when she woke up, and he missed her so much he thought it would kill him. But he was determined not to call her.

But all he could think of, all he dreamed or knew or wanted was Amanda. She was driving him crazy. And he walked down the beach at Malibu for hours on Sunday morning. He swam, and then he ran, and then he just sat there, looking out to sea, thinking of her, and he knew he couldn't stand it. He had to call her.

He fought with himself about it all that afternoon, and at eight o'clock that night, he called her. He didn't even know what to say. He just wanted to hear her voice again. Just for a minute. But he wasn't going to see her. There was no point now. He didn't want to get sucked into this insanity she was creating.

But when he got through, her machine was on, and she didn't pick up. She didn't even know he had called until the next morning when she checked it. She hardly ever bothered to check the machine now. For the first few days of their estrangement, she had checked it hourly. But she gave up by the weekend. It had been eight days now. But finally, he had reached out to her. She almost couldn't believe it. She'd begun to think that he had vanished out of her life forever. She listened to the message, and he sounded strained and uncomfortable. He said he just wanted to make sure she was okay, and feeling well. And then he had hung up. She erased the message and went back to bed. All she wanted to do was sleep now. She was exhausted. She remembered that from her earlier pregnancies, only it was worse this time. She was even more tired. She wasn't sure if it was her age, or the fact that Jack had left her. But whatever it was, she slept eighteen hours a day now.

She never returned his call, and by Tuesday, he wondered if she had gotten the message. Maybe her machine wasn't working. This time he dialed her from the office, between meetings. And he said almost the same thing he had said the first time. She heard it late that night, and wondered why he was calling. Why bother? He had made his position clear. She never wanted to see him again, or talk to him. She cried while she listened to it and went back to bed with a bowl of ice cream. That was all she ate now.

The only calls she did return were from her daughters. She didn't want them to drop by, so she figured she'd better call them. She told them she had a terrible virus, and was taking antibiotics and she'd get back to them when she felt better. Neither of them believed her.

"She's lying," Louise said when she called Jan on Tuesday. "She sounds fine, physically. Maybe she's having a nervous breakdown."

"Why don't we just leave her alone?" Jan suggested. But that night she told Paul she thought the romance was over. He thought so too. His father was behaving like Godzilla.

"I ran into him this afternoon. He looks like he hasn't combed his hair in a week, and he acts like he's going to kill someone. I think she dumped him."

"Maybe he dumped her," Jan said sadly, wondering if it was their fault, and feeling guilty about it. Her mother didn't deserve what they had done to her, but there was nothing they could do now.

And when the cleaning lady came she found Amanda watching daytime television. She had become addicted to the soap operas and talk shows where women cried about their husbands who were sleeping with the neighbor, a German shepherd, and at least two of their sisters. She watched them, and cried, while eating ice cream.

"I'm going to get fat," she announced to the television set one afternoon, eating her second bowl of ice cream. "So what?" she answered. She was going to get very, very fat, and no one decent was ever going to speak to her again. And Jack Watson was a bastard. He was probably back to sleeping with starlets.

But instead, Jack was still shouting at Gladdie and making everyone miserable. It had been nearly two weeks now.

"Look, could you do me a favor," Gladdie said finally on Friday afternoon after two weeks of his insane behavior. "Could you at least talk to her? Maybe you two can work something out. If not, you're going to drive the rest of us crazy. This entire office is becoming candidates for Prozac, thanks to you. Just call her."

"What makes you think I'm not talking to her?" he asked sheepishly, wondering how Gladdie always knew everything. He thought she was psychic.

"Have you looked at yourself lately, Jack? You shave twice a week. God knows when you last combed your hair. You've worn the same suit for three days. You're starting to look like a homeless person. Believe me, this look is not good for business."

"I'm sorry. I've been upset," he said, looking as miserable as he felt. This was almost worse than when he lost Dori. Because Amanda was right here, only minutes away, and he still loved her. That was the bitch of it. But he had behaved like a monster to her, and she hadn't returned any of his phone calls. He had called four times now. "Besides, she doesn't want to talk to me," he said sadly, and Gladdie patted his shoulder like a mother.

"Believe me, she does. She probably looks worse than you do. What did you do to her anyway?" She figured it was his fault, or he wouldn't be feeling so guilty.

"You don't want to know," he said, shamefaced.

"Probably not," Gladdie admitted. "Why don't you go over and see her?"

"She won't let me in. Why should she? I walked off on her when she needed me. . . . I threatened her, Glad. . . . I was a total asshole."

"She probably loves you anyway. Women are like that. They have a lot of tolerance for assholes. In fact, some women even love them. Go see her."

"I can't." He looked like a kid as Gladdie shook her head in exasperation.

"I'll drive you. Just do it."

"Okay, okay. I'll go tomorrow."

"Now," she said, closing his appointment book. "You don't have any appointments, and no one here can stand you. Do everyone a favor. Go see her. Or I'm starting a petition."

"You're a pain in the ass." He grinned at her and stood up. He looked better already. "But I love you." He looked down at her fondly. "Thank you. If she slams the door in my face, or won't let me in, I'll be back in ten minutes."

"I'm going to start lighting candles," she said, as he rushed through the door, anxious to get there, to see her, to tell her what he'd been thinking, and praying that she'd see him. He was at her house in less than five minutes in the Ferrari. And he rang the doorbell forever, but she didn't answer. He wasn't sure if she was home. The garage door was locked, so he couldn't see if her car was in it. But he walked around the house and started knocking on her bedroom windows.

And as she lay in bed, watching *Oprah*, she heard it.

She thought it was a bird at first, or a cat, and then she began to panic. She thought it might be a burglar, checking to see if anyone was home. She was going to call 911, and then she decided to go to her bathroom window and see if she could see someone by peeking through the curtains. She tiptoed into the other room, holding her panic button to the security system, and then she saw him. He looked terrible, and he was still tapping on her window.

She opened the bathroom window then, and stuck her head out. "What are you doing?" She looked as bad as he did. She hadn't bothered to comb her hair in days, it was just pulled back and stuffed into an elastic, and she hadn't worn makeup since she last saw him. "Stop that!" she shouted at him. "You're going to break the window."

"Then let me in," he said, smiling at her. It was so good to see her, but she only shook her head. She looked miserable, and he thought her face looked a little fuller. She actually looked very pretty.

"I don't want to see you," she said, slamming the window shut, and he came to stand at the bathroom window then, and they looked at each other through the windowpanes. She couldn't believe how much she still loved him, and how glad she was to see him. She hated herself for it. "Go away!" she mouthed, making shooing gestures, but he pressed his face against the glass and made terrible faces, and in spite of herself, she laughed at him.

"Come on, Amanda, please." He begged her, and she thought about it for a minute, and then disappeared. He had no idea what she was doing. But a minute later, she came through the back door, barefoot and wearing a nightgown. His heart leapt when he saw her.

"What time do you go to bed now?" It was four in the afternoon, and he remembered the nightgown, though with him, she hadn't worn them often.

"I went to bed two weeks ago. And I've been there ever since, eating ice cream and watching *Oprah*. I'm going to become fat and disgusting and I don't give a damn," she said as he followed her into her kitchen. And then she turned to look at him. There was something so vulnerable in her eyes that it touched him to his very soul, and he wondered again how he could have been stupid enough to leave her. "Why did you come to see me?" she asked, with a ravaged look that tore his heart out.

"Because I love you, and I'm a moron . . . and Gladdie made me." He smiled sheepishly as he said it. "She said no one can stand me. I've been pretty awful. Why didn't you return my phone calls?" He looked hurt when he asked her and she shrugged and opened the freezer.

"Do you want some ice cream?" she asked distractedly. It was becoming an obsession, and it amused him. It reminded him of eating ice cream with her in bed. Their favorite flavor was coffee. "All I have left is vanilla."

"That's pathetic. Have you eaten anything else for the last two weeks?" he asked with a look of concern, and she shook her head as she dished up two bowls of vanilla. "That's not good for the baby."

"What do you care?" She looked him straight in the eye as she said it. "That's a little hypocritical, isn't it? Since you wanted me to kill it." She handed him the bowl and they both sat down at the kitchen table.

"I didn't want you to *kill* it. I was just trying to preserve my sanity, and our life . . . at your expense. . . ." He finished sadly. "I was an asshole. I'm sorry, Amanda." He pushed the bowl of ice cream away, and just sat across the table from her as she watched him. "I was just so shocked, I didn't expect that." It was the understatement of all time and she smiled at him.

"Neither did I." At one blow, she had lost the man and gained the baby, neither of which she either wanted or expected. "I'm so sorry, Jack." He reached across the table and took her hand in his.

"It's not your fault . . . not entirely any-way. . . ." He knew she hadn't misled him. It had never occurred to either of them, not with any seri-ousness at least, that she might get pregnant. They had just dismissed it. "How are you feeling?"

"Fat," she laughed. "I must have gained five pounds eating ice cream."

"You don't look it." But there was a softness about her face, a different light in her eyes. He remem-bered that about his ex-wife when she'd been preg-nant with their kids. There was a kind of glow about her. "You look beautiful."

"It must be the hairdo." She smiled sadly. Just seeing him like this reminded her of how much she missed him. She still didn't know why he had come to see her, and she assumed it was so they could part without hard feelings. At least it was a cleaner way to do it. And maybe one day, in spite of himself, he'd come to see the baby.

"I don't suppose you'd want to go out to dinner with me . . . maybe to 31 Flavors, or Ben & Jerry's?" he asked, looking sheepish.

"Why?" What was the point now?

"Because I miss you. I've been completely crazy

for the past two weeks. It's a wonder Gladdie didn't leave me."

"I haven't been so great either. I just sleep all day, and eat ice cream. And cry at daytime television."

"I wish I'd been here."

"So do I," she said softly, and looked away from him. It was almost too painful to see him, as he stood up and walked around the table.

"I love you, Amanda . . . I want to come back, if you'll have me. I promise I won't be a jerk about this. I'll do whatever you want. You can have the baby. I'll buy it shoes. I'll buy you ice cream. I just don't want to lose you." There were tears in his eyes as he said it, and she looked up at him, unable to believe what she was hearing.

"Do you mean that?"

"About the ice cream? I swear it . . . yes, I mean it. I'm not going to leave you alone to go through this. I think you're crazy, but I love you, and it's my baby too, God help me. Just don't laugh at me when I get confused and push the stroller into the traffic because my Alzheimer's is out of control. Get me a nurse if I need one."

"I'll get you anything you want," she said as she stood up and he took her in his arms, and held her. "I love you so much. I thought I would die without you."

"Me too," he said, and pulled her closer. "God, Amanda . . . I don't want to lose you." And then,

looking worried about it, he asked her if she thought
they should get married.

"You don't have to do that," she said, shaking her
head as they walked slowly toward her bedroom. "I
don't expect it."

"No, but maybe the kid does. Maybe we should
ask him."

"Maybe it's a girl."

"Let's not talk about it. You're making me nervous. So are we getting married?" He was prepared
to do right by her, whatever it took him, but she
surprised him.

"Let's not. We don't have to. There's no law that
says we have to be married. Maybe later. Let's see
how it goes with us."

"You're very modern, Mrs. Kingston."

"No, I just love you." They were in her bedroom
by then and he had his arms around her and he was
kissing her. He was back, and she was never going to
let him go now, and before they knew it, her nightgown was on the floor, with his clothes, and they
were in bed where they had first made love, and
where they had probably conceived their baby. It
was his bed now, theirs, not Matthew's, or anyone
else's. And as he made love to her, he knew with
utter certainty, how much he loved her.

And as they lay in each other's arms that night,
they talked about what they were going to do, and
how they were going to tell their children.

"I can hardly wait," he laughed. "If you thought

the last dinner was bad, wait for this one." She had to laugh about it too. It was all you could do. And then she turned to him with a smile and asked him how much he loved her. "More than you'll ever know, more than life itself. Why? What did you have in mind?"

"I was just wondering if you loved me enough to get me a bowl of ice cream." He looked at her and laughed, and propped himself up on one elbow.

"Maybe we should just move the freezer into the bedroom."

"That's a great idea." She laughed at him, and he kissed her again, and it was a while before either of them remembered the ice cream.

Chapter Ten

This time they decided not to delude themselves, and pretend that their children were going to be happy for them. And Amanda decided, when she planned it with Jack, not to make dinner for them. They were going to invite them over for cocktails. It was going to be short and to the point, and probably horrible. But they were going to tell their children collectively that she was pregnant. And then the roof would fall in. But at least this time they both expected it.

Everyone arrived at six-fifteen. Julie was sweet when she came in, both Jan and Louise were tense, and Paul was more pleasant than usual to his father. They had already discussed it amongst themselves, and they were braced for it. They figured that Jack and Amanda were telling them they were getting married. They weren't pleased about it, and Louise had already said she was going to try to talk her out of it. But at least they knew what to expect now.

They all sat down in the living room. Jack served drinks. He poured himself a Scotch, and the others drank wine. Amanda had nothing. And Louise had water. And she decided to take the bull by the horns while the others waited politely.

"Okay," she said, looking glib, "when's the wedding?"

"It isn't," Amanda said calmly. "We're not getting married. Not for the moment anyway. We've decided to wait. But we wanted you to know, I'm pregnant." You could have heard a pin drop in the room, and Louise turned the color of chalk as she stared at her mother.

"Tell me you're joking. It's April Fools' and I forgot to look at my calendar. Tell me you didn't say that."

"I did. It came as a shock to us too. But there it is. There's no point hiding from it. It's due in October." She glanced over at Jack and he gave her thumbs-up. She was doing fine, and it took a full five minutes for it to hit them.

"I take it you're not having an abortion." As usual, Louise was the spokesperson for the two sisters. Jan had been shocked into silence. And this time, even Julie was quiet. Paul was looking daggers at his father.

"No, I'm not having an abortion. We discussed it," she said, skimming the truth a bit, "but I don't want to. At my age, this is kind of a gift, and I want to keep it. I know how difficult this will be for all of you, and it stunned me too. But there it is, guys . . . I'm human." There were tears in her eyes, and Jack walked across the room and sat down next to her and put an arm around her.

"I think your mother has a lot of courage. A lot of women her age wouldn't do this."

"I think my mother has a screw loose," Louise said as she stood up and signaled to her husband, who got up absently. "You're nuts, Mom. I think you're both senile. You'll go to any lengths to embarrass us. I don't even want to think what Daddy would say about this. It's beyond thinking."

"Well, Louise, he's not here to think anything about it. This is my life," Amanda said calmly.

"And ours, for all you care about it." But before she had even finished her sentence, they all heard Jan sobbing, and she was on her feet too, and looking at her mother with hatred.

"I can't believe you'd do this to me, Mom. I can't have a baby, so you show off to everyone that you can still have one. How cruel is that? And how rotten? How could you do this to us?" It was obvious from the look on Paul's face that he agreed with his wife completely. Both of Amanda's children and their spouses started to leave without saying another word, and Jan was distraught and leaning against her husband. Amanda tried to go to her, but Paul stopped her.

"Why don't you leave us alone for once, and just keep all your good news to yourselves for a change? What do you want from us? Blood? Congratulations? Well, screw you both. How do you think Jan is feeling?"

"I can see how she's feeling, Paul," Amanda said with tears running down her face. "The last thing on earth I wanted to do was hurt her. But this happened to us. It's our lives, and our problem, and our baby."

"Well, good luck with it. And don't invite us to the christening, Dad." He glanced at Jack with open fury. "We're not coming." The door slammed rapidly behind them, and Amanda cried in Jack's arms, as Julie watched them. She was quiet this time, and when Amanda settled down, she spoke to both of them. But it was obvious that she was still startled.

"I'm sorry, Dad. I'm sorry for both of you. This can't be easy. But it's hard for us too. It's kind of a big leap for all of us. But who knows, maybe in the end it will be a blessing. I hope so."

"So do I," Jack said softly, looking at Amanda. She had certainly taken a tough route when she made her decision, but she knew that. And they had expected it to be rough when they told the children. Julie and her husband left quietly. And Jack and Amanda sat staring at each other in silence.

"You knew it would be like this," he said gently.

"I know," she sniffed. "But you always hope it

won't be. You always think they'll jump up and throw their arms around you, like they did when they were kids, little kids, and tell you how much they love you, and it's okay, and they think you're terrific. Instead, they're always passing judgment, and angry at you, and think that whatever it is you're doing is wrong and you did it to hurt them. It's as if your only function in life, as a parent, is to exist in whatever way they want you. Anything different, or out of the ordinary, or inconvenient, just makes them angry. Why is it that children, however old they are, *never* have compassion for their parents?"

"Maybe we don't deserve it," he said, looking tired. "Maybe they just think we're selfish. And we are sometimes. But we have a right to that. We give them so much when they're little, and when we think it's finally our turn, they turn around and tell us it isn't. We don't have a turn. As far as they're concerned, we're on their time. I think you just have to do what you're doing, and make your own life. If they can live with it, fine. If they can't, let them deal with it. We can't give up the rest of our lives for our children. The only thing that depresses me is that we're about to do it all over again. I'm going to slide right into the sunset with some little shit telling me what an asshole I am, and how I ruined his life because I'm still sleeping with his mother. And believe me, I will be. I plan to be making love to you until they put me away with a shovel, and if you ever get pregnant again, next time, I swear I'll never sleep with you again. I want you on birth control pills till you're eighty." She couldn't help laughing at what he said, some of it was so true. One's children always seem to think that you owe them everything, and they owe you nothing. It was an interesting concept.

"I felt so badly for Jan," she said solemnly. What she had said had been so agonized and so painful.

"So did I. Paul looked as though he wanted to kill me. It's as though we did this so I could prove my virility and make him look bad. Christ, I would do anything to see them have a baby."

"So would I," she said, and then to take their minds off all of it, he took her to dinner. But for the moment, they had given up Thai food. Amanda couldn't even think about it without getting heartburn.

And that night, they lay in bed and talked for a long time. Jack fell asleep eventually, but Amanda didn't. She got up and made some hot milk, and drank chamomile tea, but her mind seemed to be whirling. She kept thinking about Jan and what she had said. Amanda slept fitfully all night, and the next day, she looked at Jack mournfully over breakfast.

"I have something to say to you," she said, and he glanced up at her. She looked tired.

"Are you okay?" He always worried about her, and now he worried about the baby. This was just what he hadn't wanted.

"I'm fine," she reassured him. But she didn't look it. She looked awful. "I had an idea last night."

"In your condition that could be dangerous. You probably want me to buy out Häagen-Dazs, or Ben & Jerry's."

"I'm serious."

"So am I. I'm buying stock in the companies. You are the single biggest consumer of ice cream west of the Rockies." She had already gained eight pounds and was barely three months pregnant. "Okay, okay, I'll be serious. What is it?"

She started to cry before she even told him, and he realized instantly that it was serious. But she talked about Jan and Paul and what they had said the night before, and how greatly it had pained her.

"Sweetheart, it upset me too. But there's nothing we can do about it. They just have to see what happens, and keep trying."

"Maybe not. That was my idea. You didn't want this baby anyway, Jack. And maybe we are too old. Maybe this is the greatest gift we can give them. Maybe this is why it happened. I want to give them the baby." He looked stunned when she said it.

"Are you serious? You want to give them the baby?" She nodded as she cried, and he put his arms around her.

"I don't think you should do that. This is your baby. Our baby. It would be so hard for you to give it up once you had it."

"I don't care. I want to do this for Jan, and for Paul. Will you let me?"

"You can do anything you want. It's an extraordinary thing to do, and people will talk about it. But who gives a damn? If that's what you want, and what they want, then do it."

"I wanted to ask you first."

He nodded. "I think it's the greatest gift you can give them, and since Paul is so opposed to adoption, it certainly solves the issue of the genes. I just want you to be sure you can do it."

"I know I can. I want to. If it's all right with you, I want to talk to her this morning. Will you call Paul?"

"All right, I'll take him to lunch. If he'll see me."

"I'll have Jan call him after I talk to her, and tell him this is important."

"You're an amazing woman, sweetheart. And full of surprises and rare gifts." He was still amazed by her when he left for the store that morning. She didn't even bother to call Jan. She drove to her house before she left for the gallery, and Jan was so surprised, in spite of her resistance, she opened the door to her mother. And when Amanda told her what she had in mind, the two women sat and cried. At first Jan was shocked, and didn't want to do it, but after Amanda talked to her for a while, she wanted it very badly.

"Would you really do that for me, Mom?"

"Yes, I would," Amanda said firmly, drying her eyes, and smiling at her daughter. "I'd like nothing better."

"What if you change your mind? Or Jack does?"

"We won't. If we give you our word, we'll do it. This is something we both want to do. Very much. I hope you'll let us."

"I'll talk to Paul." Jan looked excited as she ran to the telephone, and was surprised to learn that Jack had already called him, and Paul already had some vague idea as to why his father wanted to see him. Jan explained the rest to him, and there were tears in his eyes as he listened.

"I can't believe they'd do that," he whispered. "Why?"

"Because they love us," Jan said, starting to cry again as her mother stood near her. "Mom says we can both be there when the baby is born, and it's ours right from that very minute."

"What if they change their minds?"

"I don't think they will, Paul. She really means it."

"We'll talk about it," he said, afraid to get his hopes up. But he saw his father for lunch, and talked to Jan about it that night, and the next morning they called their respective parents, and accepted. Their mood was jubilant, and Amanda felt as though she had done something worthwhile and wonderful, and she knew she'd never regret it.

"I can't believe you," Jack said, in awe of her. "I just hope you're not sorry later."

"I won't be. I'm absolutely sure. I don't care how much I love this baby once it's born, they should have it. You were probably right anyway. Maybe I will be too old to carpool at sixty."

"You'd be cute at any age. And at least you can see the baby whenever you want to." That was something. He knew this wouldn't be easy for her. And then he had an idea. "Why don't we go away somewhere? Just the two of us, for a vacation. What about Paris?"

"Wow! I'd love that." The girls had suggested it to her the summer before, but she hadn't been in the mood then. But she couldn't think of anything she'd like more than a trip to Paris with Jack Watson.

They went in June when she was five and a half months pregnant. They stayed at the Ritz and had a fabulous time. They went out for dinner every night, shopped, went to the Louvre and the ballet, and walked all over Paris. She had never felt better. In spite of the ice cream, she hadn't gained much weight, and Jack thought she looked terrific. Everything they said about pregnant women being beautiful seemed to hold true for her. The only thing she was sorry about was that she couldn't buy really great clothes while she was pregnant.

"We'll come back in November, I promise." He was worried that she'd be depressed then. He still thought that giving up the baby would be hard for her, but she had never wavered once in her resolve to give it to their children.

They had a terrific time, and stopped in London for a few days on the way home. And in July he took her to Lake Tahoe. But in August, her doctor told her she couldn't travel. She was seven and a half months pregnant, and she was hardly a young mother. The baby was large, and the doctor was afraid it would come early.

"My others were both late," she said confidently, and her obstetrician laughed at her openly.

"And how old were you then?"

"All right, all right. I'll be good. I promise."

They knew that the baby was healthy, and a boy, she had had amniocentesis before they went to Europe. And Jan and Paul were going crazy over names. Louise, on the other hand, was still being silent and had scarcely spoken to her mother.

"She'll get over it," Jack reassured her. He just wanted her to be happy. And he did everything he could to distract her. But all she thought of now was the baby. She wanted to buy clothes for it, teddy bears, cribs and tiny little underwear, and mountains of diapers. She seemed to go shopping almost daily, and whenever possible, she insisted he come with her.

"What are people going to think, for God's sake? I look like the baby's grandfather." He was still mortified every time she took him shopping, and whenever someone asked, he said what they were buying was for their grandchild.

"What does that make me? Your daughter?"

"How about my wife? You know, that could be arranged." They had been going out for eight months by then, but whenever he said it, she ignored him. She didn't want to think about anything at the moment, except the baby. She even made Jack come to the doctor with her.

The first time he had gone had been mortifying, and he had wanted to crawl out the door with a mask on. Instead, he had held the newspaper over his face, and tried to pretend he didn't know her.

"I'm not going in," he whispered from behind the *Los Angeles Times*. Everyone in the waiting room looked about fourteen to him. It looked like a summer camp for unwed mothers. They were all pretty girls from Beverly Hills with blond hair and short dresses. They looked as though they'd been taking candy from strangers.

"Don't be ridiculous. All they do is listen to the heartbeat. It's exciting," she whispered back to him, and he peeked around the paper. There was a boy in blue jeans across from him. He looked like a child actor.

"You can tell me about it. I'll wait for you in the car," he said firmly. But she looked so devastated when he tried to leave, that he sat down again with a mortified expression, and the boy in the blue jeans asked him if it was his first baby. "My children are older than you are," Jack said miserably. The boy said he was twenty-three, it was their second child. But his father and stepmother had had one the year before.

"He's sixty-five," the boy said with a broad smile.

"Did he survive it?"

"Yeah. They had twins. In vitro. They tried for two years. My stepmom is forty."

"Lucky devils," Jack said wryly, and then said to Amanda in the examining room that people were crazy. "Why would a sixty-five-year-old man *want* to have a baby? Imagine doing this 'in vitro.' At least we had a good time when we did it."

"Want to try again?" she teased him, and he rolled his eyes. But when the doctor handed the stethoscope to him and he heard the baby's heartbeat, even Jack was excited. It was suddenly so real that it brought tears to his eyes.

"That's my grandchild!" he said, too loud, because the stethoscope in his ears made him think he was speaking softly, which he wasn't.

"Is this your father?" the doctor asked her then, looking confused. "I thought he was your husband."

"Actually, my husband died a year and a half ago," she explained, and the doctor smiled at her benignly. Like all the people in Beverly Hills, these people were clearly more than a little eccentric.

But the baby was fine, and Jack couldn't stop talking about it all the way back to Julie's.

"Next time we should really bring Jan and Paul," he said, and Amanda agreed with him, pleased that he was excited about the baby. She had to see the doctor nearly every week now. He wanted to keep a close eye on her. He was still concerned that she might deliver early, and to Jack at least, her belly looked enormous. He couldn't remember either of his children being that size in utero, but Amanda was also very slender, so it showed more.

But the very worst experience for him was the Lamaze classes they began on the fifteenth of August. There were twelve couples, mostly in shorts, beards, and Birkenstocks, lying on the floor of a conference room at Cedars Sinai. Jack had come from a meeting at the office in a Brioni suit and shirt and tie, and they looked at him like a visitor from another planet. Amanda was already there, waiting for him, and she looked very relaxed in white shorts and a huge pink T-shirt and sandals. She had just had her nails done, and she looked like a model. The people there were too young to even realize she had ever been an actress. Outside, the temperature was blazing, and Jack looked hot and frazzled when he got there.

"Sorry I'm late, sweetheart. I couldn't get rid of the textile guys from Paris. They wanted to schmooze forever."

"It's fine," she whispered with a smile, "they just started." There were charts on the wall showing varying stages of a woman's dilated cervix. And Jack glanced over at it with horror.

"What is that?"

"A cervix. Dilated. Don't worry about it."

"It looks awful." He had spent the arrival of both his children in a bar, getting drunk with a friend. In those days, fathers didn't have to do anything more exotic than show up afterward, with flowers.

He glanced around the room then, and realized that, as usual, almost everyone there was the age of his children. But he was almost used to that by then. What he was not used to were the photographs they showed, or the diagrams, or the training film they had promised at the end of the session. He was looking grimmer by the second.

The only part he found even remotely bearable, though embarrassing, were the exercises he had to do with Amanda, holding her legs, or helping her breathe. And the woman at the front of the room talked constantly about the miseries of something called "transition."

"What is *that*?" he said to his "wife" after the sixth time she'd said it. But he had said it too loudly, and the instructor had heard him.

"It's the most painful part of labor," she said with a sadistic smile, "when you go from this . . ." she pointed to a chart ". . . to this. It's a little bit like taking your upper lip and pulling it over the top of your head." She moved on to the next question.

"Doesn't this scare you?" he whispered, a lot more softly this time, to Amanda.

"No, it's fine," she whispered back. "I've been through it."

"Did you do it without drugs?" The woman at the front of the room kept warning them about the evils of anesthesia, and had made it clear that "real" women didn't ask for medication.

"Of course not." Amanda grinned at him between puffing breaths and panting. "They can give me everything they've got. In the parking lot preferably. I'm no hero."

"I'm glad to hear it. What about me? Will they give me some too?" He was beginning to feel as though he was going to need it. He hated the people in the class, hated the way they looked, the things they said, and the stupid questions they asked. It was a wonder any of them had ever gotten pregnant. Apparently, even morons could do it. But what he hated most was their instructor.

And when she announced that the film today was an actual caesarean, Jack began to glance longingly toward the exits.

"Don't you want something to drink, sweetheart?" he asked casually. "It's so hot in here." Actually, the air conditioner was on, and it was freezing.

"Just close your eyes. I won't tell." The purpose of the film was so that if any of them had an emergency C-section, the husbands would be prepared and present. If they had seen it, and had a certificate from the class to prove it, they could stay in the operating room and watch. If not, they had to wait outside, with the sissies. But Jack knew that there was no way he could have been there anyway, not without general anesthesia.

"I'll be right back," he whispered, too loud again.

"Where are you going?" Amanda asked.

"To the men's room," he whispered.

"We'll wait for you, Mr. Kingston!" the voice at the front of the room proclaimed loudly. "You won't want to miss this." He gave a quelling look at his "wife," and was back in under five minutes.

And with that, they started the film that almost killed him. He had been in the army for two years as a kid, but no training film they had shown him there rivaled this one. Even the one on gonorrhea was a pleasant memory compared to what looked like the sawing in half of some poor woman. She cried through most of it, looked as though she was in terrible pain, there was blood everywhere, and before the lights came up, Jack whispered to Amanda that he was nauseous.

"I told you. Don't look." She squeezed his hand and leaned over to kiss him.

"Kingstons!" The voice from hell sliced through the room. "Are you paying attention? There will be a brief quiz on this subject."

"Shit. Why can't we watch them operating on hemorrhoids?"

"Shhhh . . ." Amanda was laughing at him. He was hopeless. They never went back again. She didn't want natural childbirth anyway. She had tried it for about an hour with Louise, and she knew better.

But the last weeks of her pregnancy seemed very easy to her. On Labor Day weekend, she was eight months pregnant, and bored to death. They had gone to a movie, eaten Chinese food, and walked down the beach at Malibu, which was not quite as easy as it had been. She felt fine, but she was slow now and enormous.

They were sitting on his deck, drinking iced tea, when Paul called them. He wanted to know how Amanda was, and asked if they could come by later. And Jack said, when he hung up, that Paul sounded a little nervous.

"Do you think something's wrong?" Amanda asked, looking worried.

"I don't think so. Maybe they're just getting anxious about the baby."

"So am I," she said unconvincingly. She had been remarkably calm all through it. "If this thing gets any bigger I won't fit into the elevator at Cedars Sinai."

"Boys are like that," Jack said with a smile. "Paul was a big baby too. His mother was mad at me for six months. She was such a little darling."

"She gave you great kids," Amanda reminded him charitably, and he rolled his eyes at her.

"Don't be such a good guy. She was a witch, trust me."

Paul and Jan came by late that afternoon, and Jack made drinks while they sat on the deck with Amanda, watching the sunset. It was a gorgeous afternoon, and Amanda was thinking about going swimming.

"Is the baby okay?" Jan asked, looking at her mother with concern. She was so huge it was scary, but Amanda didn't seem to mind it. She looked amazingly peaceful.

"He's fine. Waiting for you, sweetheart," Amanda said with a smile, and Jack came back and handed the young people sangria. He noticed that both of them took long sips before speaking. And he wondered what was cooking.

"Something wrong?" Jack decided to break the ice, and the young couple shook their heads in unison, looking like guilty teenagers, and then laughed nervously as they looked from her mother to his father.

"No," Paul spoke for them. Jan was too nervous. "But there's something we want to tell you . . . or we thought we should anyway. You should really be the first to know. . . ."

Jan stepped in then, with tears in her eyes as she looked at her mother, "Mom, I'm pregnant."

"You are? Oh baby, how terrific. When did that happen?"

"About six weeks ago. I wanted to be sure before I told you. But the doctor has confirmed it and said I'm fine. I had a sonogram this week and everything's perfect. They even gave us a picture."

"I remember that," Jack said, looking at them. But he wondered what the rest was. There was more to this story, he knew, as he waited.

Jan and Paul both took a deep breath then, and

looked from one to the other of their parents. "I know this will probably screw up your plans, but we just don't know . . . we don't think . . . I'm not sure we should . . ."

Jack said it for them. "You don't want our baby." Amanda looked stunned as both their children shook their heads, and then qualified it.

"Unless you two really don't want to keep it. If you don't want it, then of course . . ." Paul was trying to be fair to them, but it was obvious that now that they were having their own child, they didn't want her mother's. "We're really sorry."

"That's all right, Son," Jack said calmly. "Things work out for the best sometimes. Now, why don't you two run along." He looked at his daughter-in-law and congratulated her with a kiss and a hug. "I want to talk to your mother."

"We understand. I know this must be a little hard on you, Dad." They sounded young and insensitive and unaware, and yet at the same time, he didn't blame them. And he wasn't sorry either.

"It's fine, Son."

They were gone within ten minutes, and Amanda looked as though someone had let the air out of her tires. It definitely required a shift in her thinking. She had done everything not to get attached to this child, and now suddenly it was hers again, and she had to rethink it.

"Wow, there's a quick change of pace. I'm happy for them though." She looked at Jack from where she sat, checking for a negative reaction, but there was none. He seemed fine about it. But the way things were, he had no real obligation either. "I guess that takes us back to the beginning."

"Maybe," he said noncommittally. "Why don't we just let it sink in for a day or two, and talk about it later," he suggested, and it seemed like a good idea to her. They both needed time to digest it, although her style was usually to solve problems on the instant. But this was different. This involved major life decisions. Or maybe none at all. The baby was due in four weeks. There was nothing left to decide now. And she had bought everything the baby needed, for her daughter. All she had to do now was have it. "Come on, let's take a walk down the beach." She didn't say anything, but they didn't make it far, and in a little while they came back, and she wandered into his bedroom. She had been so happy here. They had spent such good times in each other's company. And their love had grown in countless ways in the nine months they'd been together.

"Want to take a nap?" he offered casually, as he walked into the room behind her.

"I'd like that. I'm exhausted." The emotional shock of having the baby given back to them had left her feeling drained, elated in some ways, and frightened and worried in others, and more than anything, concerned about Jack's reaction. It had been such a perfect solution for them, and they'd both been comfortable with it. "Are you going to leave me again?" she asked in a soft voice, trying not to sound as frightened as she was, as the setting sun was framed in the picture window in his bedroom.

"Of course not. I love you . . . and I love him . . . poor little guy, he's getting kicked around like a football."

"From where I sit, it feels like he's doing all the kicking." Jack loved feeling him move and kick and dance around. Sometimes when she lay against him as she slept it made him smile just to feel it. And he knew how worried she must be now. She didn't deserve this. And he realized again what a fool he had been from the beginning.

He lay down next to her, and very gently kissed her. "What are my chances of making love to you at this stage in the game?" They hadn't tried it in two weeks, and already by then it had been quite a challenge. She smiled when he asked her.

"The doctor says we can do it on the way to the hospital, if you want to."

"I want to." And he looked as though he meant it.

"You're a brave man," she whispered with a smile, and he peeled off her bathing suit and rubbed a hand across her belly. And at that exact moment, the baby gave a huge kick and they both laughed.

"I think he heard what I asked you, and I'm not so sure he liked it." They lay together for a while, and he held her, and eventually, their passion took over. It was gentle and slow, and better than either of them would have expected. And when Amanda fell asleep next to him, he put his bathing suit on and walked back out to the beach. There was a lot to think about, a lot to decide. And he smiled, as he glanced at her from the doorway.

Chapter Eleven

Jack cooked dinner for her that night, and he seemed very quiet to Amanda. She was afraid that he was upset about what Jan and Paul had said. But when she asked him, he said that he wasn't. He seemed very comfortable, and at peace with himself, and when they sat on the deck afterward and looked up at the stars, he reached for her hand, and leaned over to kiss her. It was a perfect evening.

"There's something I want to ask you," he said finally. She couldn't imagine what was coming. She turned to look at him with a mildly worried frown. "I did a lot of thinking this afternoon. Actually, I've done a lot of thinking lately. It just seemed so easy to let Jan and Paul take the baby. It was easier to let you make that decision."

"It seemed such a great thing to do for them."
She sounded disappointed. She still wasn't sure what
she was feeling.

"It was. You were incredible to do it. But it was
never right. Maybe whatever Powers there are knew
that, and got her pregnant." He paused, but only for
an instant. "I want us to keep the baby. He's our son
. . . I really want him." There were tears in his eyes
in the darkness, but she couldn't see them.

"You do?" For the second time that day she
looked as though someone could have knocked her
over with a feather. "Are you sure?"

"Of course I'm sure. And I'm tired of all this stupid modern bullshit. I want us to get married. Now.
Tomorrow. Immediately. I don't want our son to be
born out of wedlock."

"That still gives you four weeks." Amanda smiled
at him, wondering if he really meant it, or was just
being noble. "You don't have to do this. I love you
just as much as if we were married."

"So do I. So why not be? This is such a dumb way
to do things. I live in Malibu, and you live in Bel Air,
and we sleep together on weekends? I want to be
there for night feedings and runny noses, and his
first step and first tooth, and your first gray hair,
and . . ." He was smiling at her, and she was laughing at him.

"I hate to tell you, you've already missed it. About
ten years ago, in fact."

"Then I don't want to miss the rest. I don't know

what I've been thinking. I've been so busy protecting myself for the last twenty years, that I forgot about protecting you. More importantly, I'd forgotten how good this can be. I just don't want part of it, or the easy times. I want all of it. I want to be there if you get sick, or if you're happy, or sad, or need me. And I want you there for me too. Even if I start to drool at the same time he does." He gently touched her belly and she put his finger to her lips and kissed it.

"I want to be there for you too," she said softly. "And you have been there for me." And then suddenly, she looked worried again. "You don't think it's too soon?" But this time, he laughed out loud, and their neighbors could have heard him.

"Amanda, I love you. Have you looked at yourself? That's quite a profile. No, it's not a moment too soon. Not a minute. Let's get married next weekend. I'll call the kids, and if one of them has one lousy word to say about it, I'm going to disinherit them, and I'm going to say so. And that includes Louise! It's time those kids gave you a little support for a change, instead of just taking from you, or expecting you to accept them, and let them say anything they damn well please to you. I want to see smiles this time, and hear congratulations! They owe us this one." And she could see from the fire in his eyes that he wasn't kidding and she loved it.

And the next day, he did exactly what he said he would. He called all their kids and told them he and Amanda were getting married. The wedding was set for the following Saturday. Jack had asked an old friend, a judge, to marry them. He was going to do it at the store, and afterward they were having a reception for two hundred people. And Jack and Gladdie did everything. Much as Amanda would have hated to admit it to him, she was finally too tired to do it. She suddenly felt fourteen months pregnant, and she looked it.

He even found a dress for her, a beautiful cream-colored Gazar that fell over her vast form like petals. It was perfect. She was going to wear flowers in her hair, and carry a bouquet of tube roses, philanopsis orchids, and freesia. Both her daughters had agreed to be there, and Jack had invited them both to come to the store to pick out their dresses. Jan had come willingly, but of course Louise didn't. But she had promised Jack on the phone that on the day of the wedding, she'd be pleasant. And she was furious he'd called her. She thought her mother should have done it. She was always furious about something.

And when the day of the wedding came, Jack and Amanda took a short walk down the beach in Malibu and then she went back to her place to dress with her daughters. Both of them had agreed to help her. And she was as nervous as any bride, as her hands trembled when she slipped her dress on. The hairdresser had come to do her hair, in the smooth chignon that had been her trademark, and she looked spectacular, even eight and a half months pregnant.

"You look nice, Mom." Louise stood behind her,

and spoke to the reflection in the mirror, when Jan went downstairs to check the flowers.

"Thank you," Amanda said gratefully, and then slowly she turned to face her. "You're not too angry at me?" But even if she was, Amanda was doing exactly what she wanted.

"I'm not angry. I still miss Dad though. Even if he was a pain in the neck sometimes." Her eyes filled with tears as she said it. She had not only forgiven her mother finally, but her father.

"I miss him too, Lou." Amanda took her older daughter in her arms and held her for a moment and then pulled away to look at her. She was difficult, but essentially a decent person. "But I love Jack too."

"He's a nice guy," Louise conceded, and then her eyes clouded again. There was something she had to ask her. "Would you have done it for me, Mom? I mean give me the baby, if I couldn't have one." The question had tormented her from the beginning.

"Of course I would. I would do it for either of you."

"I always thought you loved her more. She was always so special to you." Louise's voice choked on a sob, and her mother was shocked by what she was saying.

"So were you. You're both special. I love both of you. Of course I'd have done that for you. How could you think I wouldn't?"

"Stupid, I guess. Jerry said you would when I talked to him about it."

"Then he's smarter than you are."

And then Louise surprised her even further. "I'm glad you're keeping it. It'll be good for you. It'll keep you young . . . or drive you crazy."

"Probably both." Amanda laughed through her own tears, as Jan walked into the room, and Amanda hugged Louise once more and a secret look passed between them. Nothing like that had ever happened. And then she turned to both of them, and asked them if they'd be with her when she had the baby. "I don't think Jack's going to make it. He almost threw up in Lamaze class."

Louise laughed at what she said, and looked enormously flattered. "So did Jerry. But he was fine when the time came. Maybe Jack will be too."

"I don't think his vintage does childbirth."

"Well, we'll be there." Jan put an arm through her sister's, and they both smiled at their mother.

"It won't be for another two or three weeks. Just make sure I can reach you when the time comes."

"Don't worry, Mom," they said in chorus, and with that the limousine arrived, and the photographer. And they almost forgot her bouquet. She was so nervous she was breathless, but she looked terrific. And they helped her into the car, and they were all laughing at how hard it was to get her in it. She could hardly move now.

And when they arrived at the store, all three of them were dazzled. The flowers were spectacular, and there was literally a solid ceiling of flowers above them. There were orchids and roses and lilies of the valley. It was the most beautiful thing Amanda had ever seen, and when she stood next to Jack with the judge, and her children at her side, she was suddenly overcome with emotion. It meant just as much to her, or perhaps more, as her first wedding. She was wiser now, and knew how lucky she was to have him. And at this time in their lives, they suited each other to perfection.

The judge declared them man and wife, and this time, just as Jack had requested of them, there were smiles and congratulations, and they genuinely meant it. The whole family posed for photographs, and drank Champagne, except for Amanda, who drank ginger ale. And twenty minutes later, the guests arrived. It seemed like an enormous wedding.

Everyone was still there at midnight, and Amanda was so tired that Jack didn't dare keep her there a moment longer. She threw her bouquet from the staircase, and Gladdie caught it, while George Christy wrote down names. He was the only member of the press that Jack had invited. And as they ran to the car, the staff threw petals at them. They weren't going far. They were spending two days at the Bel Air, two blocks from her house, but Amanda could hardly wait to get there and take her clothes off. It had been the happiest day of her life, but she was beyond exhausted, and she looked it. Jack put an arm around her in the car. He had insisted on driving to the Bel Air in his red Ferrari, and it was covered with balloons and white satin ribbons, and someone had written on it in shaving cream "Just Married."

"I feel like a kid again," he beamed at her. He had loved it.

"I feel like a grandmother," she laughed, "a very fat one. You and Gladdie did such a great job. It was all so perfect. I can't wait to see the pictures."

He had ordered Champagne in the room, and more ginger ale for her. There was a stack of videos, and as soon as the bellboy left he helped her take her clothes off. She could hardly move as she lay on the bed in her pantyhose and her bra. She had had a backache for hours, but she didn't want to spoil the moment and tell him. She lay back on the bed with a happy sigh, and let her head fall back in a mountain of down pillows.

"Oh my God . . . I've died and gone to heaven . . ." she said with a smile, and he looked down at her, a happy man. This was everything he wanted. The past was gone now.

"Can I get you anything?" he asked, as he took off his tie.

"A forklift," she grinned at him. "I'm never going to be able to get up if I have to go to the bathroom."

"I'll carry you," he said gallantly.

"It would kill you."

He dropped his suit on a chair, and came to lie beside her, drinking Champagne and eating the strawberries and truffles the hotel had left at their bedside. "Try one of these," he said, putting a choc-olate in her mouth, and she sighed contentedly, as he started to flip through the movies. "How about a porno?"

"I'm not sure I'm up to it," she laughed.

"On our wedding night?" He looked disap-pointed.

"We don't have to do that anymore. We're mar-ried." He grinned at her, and put a movie on, and it was so awful, she laughed at it with him. But when he got amorous, she looked at him with a mournful expression. "Baby, I'd like to, but I don't think I can even take the rest of my clothes off."

"I'll help you," he said hopefully, but she could see that he had had a lot of wine, and she didn't take him seriously, as she lumbered out of bed and went to the bathroom. She had been a thousand times that night, and lying on the bed her backache had gotten worse instead of better.

"I think I'll take a shower," she said from the bathroom doorway.

"Now?" It was one o'clock in the morning, but somehow she thought it might make her feel better. She was beyond exhausted. She hated to feel so rot-ten on their wedding night, but it had been a long day and a long night. And she had been on her feet for hours. They felt like footballs.

But the shower made her feel better, and when she came back to the bedroom, they were still going at it on TV, and Jack was snoring softly. She sat down on the bed for a minute and just looked at him, thinking about how odd life was. How life put you together with different people at different times. She couldn't imagine being with anyone but him now.

He stirred slightly as she slipped into bed next to him, and a minute later, she turned the light and the TV off. But as soon as she lay down, the baby started kicking. It was going to be a long night at this rate, she thought to herself. She lay there for what seemed like ages, but she couldn't sleep. She still had the backache, and now along with it, she felt a very odd kind of pressure, as though the baby was pushing his head downward. And then suddenly, a twinge at the very bottom of her belly struck a chord of memory. She was in labor. And the twinges were contractions.

They were mild at first. And she noticed that it was fully ten minutes before she had the next one. They were slow and steady and regular, and at three in the morning, as she still lay in the dark next to him, they were coming every five minutes. She wasn't sure if she should wake him. It seemed silly if it was too early. But he heard her when she went to the bathroom.

"You okay?" he muttered sleepily when she came back to bed and moved closer to him.

"I think I'm having the baby," she whispered.

He sat bolt upright. *"Now? Here?* I'll call the doctor." He instantly flipped the light on, and they both squinted.

"I don't think it's time yet." But as soon as she

said it, she had a good hard pain that made her grit her teeth and writhe beside him. But it was over in less than a minute.

"Are you crazy? Do you want to have the baby here?" He jumped out of bed and put his pants on, and she was laughing at him when the next pain came. But suddenly they were coming every two minutes.

"I haven't even unpacked my suitcase," she said between pains. "I wanted to spend at least one night here."

"I'll bring you back here, I swear, after we have the baby. Anytime you want. Now get your ass out of bed so we can get to the doctor before you have this baby."

"I meant I have nothing to wear."

"What's wrong with what you were wearing?"

"I can't wear my wedding dress to the hospital. I'll look silly."

"I won't tell anyone what it is. Just get dressed, Amanda, for God's sake. . . . What are you doing? . . ."

"I'm having a contraction," she said between clenched teeth again, and almost as soon as she did he clutched his stomach.

"I think the Champagne was poisoned."

"Maybe you're in labor too," she said when the pain stopped. "Call Jan and Louise," she said, crawling out of bed. But she was having a hard time standing up now.

"I'll call an ambulance."

"I don't *want* an ambulance." She was trapped between laughter and tears when the next pain came. "You drive me."

"I can't. I'm blind drunk. Can't you see that?"

"No, you look fine to me. Then I'll drive. Just call Jan and Louise."

"I don't know their numbers, and if you don't put your damn wedding dress on right now, I'm calling the police and having you arrested."

"That would be nice," she said in muffled tones as she slipped the wedding dress over her head and clutched her stomach. But when she tried to put her shoes on, she found her feet were too swollen. "I'll have to go barefoot," she said practically.

"For God's sake . . . Amanda . . . please . . ." He threw her suitcase on the bed, and started pawing through it. And miraculously, he found a pair of slippers. "Put these on."

"What is it about you people in retail? Why couldn't I just go barefoot?"

"You'd look foolish." They were standing in the doorway of the room by then, and it was just after four o'clock in the morning, but the next pain was so hard that she had to lean against the doorway. Just watching her, Jack started to moan, and she put an arm around him as they left the room and walked slowly to the front of the hotel, where he had parked the car. It felt as if it took forever to get there. In truth, it took more than ten minutes, and she was beginning to worry that she'd have the baby before they ever reached the Ferrari.

She slipped into the driver's seat, and held her hand out to him, praying that he had remembered to bring the keys. She didn't want to wait a minute longer. But fortunately, they were in his pocket. And he handed them over to her, and slipped into the car beside her. And as they careened out of the parking lot through Bel Air, she gave him Jan's number and told him to call her.

"Tell her to call Louise. Just tell them to meet me there, in labor and delivery. We'll be there in five minutes."

"They'll probably send me to geriatrics."

"Just relax, you'll be fine," she said, smiling at him. It was a hell of a way to spend a honeymoon. Any minute they were going to have a baby. So much so, that she had to pull off the road for the next contraction.

"Oh my God," he screamed at her, "what are you doing?"

"I'm trying not to wreck your Ferrari while I have a contraction," she said, sounding more like the girl in *The Exorcist* than the woman he had just married, and he looked at her in horror.

"Shit! I think you're in transition!"

"Don't tell me what I'm in, just shut up and call my goddamn daughter."

"That's it . . . that's it . . . that's what the monster at the hospital said . . . she said you'd start behaving like someone I don't even know. *That's* transition!" She wasn't sure if she wanted to laugh or kill him. But at least he called Jan then, and announced that her mother was in transition.

"Is this a joke?" Jan asked, she'd been sound asleep and she didn't know what he was talking about. It was obvious he had had too much to drink at the wedding.

"Of course this isn't a joke," he shouted into the phone, sounding hysterical. "She's having the baby and we're on the way to the hospital, and she's in transition. She sounds like a total stranger."

"Are you sure it's Mom?" Jan laughed at him. He was an even bigger mess than her mother had predicted.

"Well, she's wearing your mother's wedding dress at least. And she wants you to call Louise. But hurry!"

"We'll be there in ten minutes!" she said, and hung up just as Amanda screeched into the hospital driveway, and threw open the door to the Ferrari, with an exasperated look at her brand-new husband.

"You park it. I'm busy. And don't scratch the car, my husband will kill you."

"Very funny, lady. Very funny, whoever you are. Looks just like my wife too," he said to a night guard, who shook his head and pointed to where Jack could park it. He figured they were probably on drugs, everyone in L.A. was.

Amanda was already in the lobby by then, and

sitting in a wheelchair. She had given them her doctor's name, and just as they had learned in Lamaze, she was panting and blowing. The contractions were getting ugly.

"What are you doing?" Jack asked as he looked at her, and then he remembered. "I forgot my stopwatch." But a nurse was already wheeling her into the elevator, as she clutched the arms of the wheelchair. She was making Jack very nervous. "Baby, are you okay? . . . I mean really . . ."

"What does it look like?" Her voice was barely audible through the contraction, but she sounded a little more like herself now. Maybe she wasn't in transition.

"It looks miserable," he said honestly, "worse than that."

"It *is* worse than that. It's like having your guts ripped open with a chain saw."

"What happened to the thing with the upper lip?"

"That comes later."

"I can hardly wait."

They wheeled her into a room on the third floor, and she exchanged her clothes for a faded hospital gown, and they handed Jack a shower cap and a pair of green pajamas.

"What's that for?" He looked panicked.

"You, if you want to see your baby born," the nurse told him without ceremony, and then called for a resident to check Amanda.

He appeared in the labor room two minutes later,

while Jack was changing, and announced that Amanda was at eight centimeters and going fast. She was at nine by the time he was finished.

"Get me an epidural," she said, clutching the bars on the side of the bed through the next contraction . . . "morphine . . . Demerol . . . anything . . . give me something. . . ."

"It's too late, Mrs. Kingston," the nurse said soothingly. "You should have been here at seven centimeters."

"I was busy. I was driving to the hospital in my husband's fucking Ferrari." She was crying then. This wasn't funny. And she turned around to look at the resident and the nurse with fury. "Are you telling me that if I had been here half an hour ago, I could have had an epidural? This is *your* fault," she said to Jack miserably as he emerged from the bathroom looking like a scrub nurse.

"What's my fault? Oh this . . ." he looked at the enormous belly, "I guess it is. And by the way," he turned to the doctor imperiously, "she's not Mrs. Kingston."

"She's not?" He looked startled and picked up the chart. It said it plainly. "It says here she's Mrs. Kingston."

"She's Mrs. Watson," Jack corrected, still drunk from the unknown quantities of Champagne he had drunk at their wedding.

It was going to be hours, possibly days, before he was sober, and Amanda knew it.

"Never mind who I am. Just get my doctor. Where is he?"

"I'm right here, Amanda," a voice from the doorway said coolly.

"Good. I want drugs, and they won't give them to me." He talked to the resident for a minute and then nodded.

"How about a little morphine?"

"Sounds terrific." They attached her to a monitor, gave her the shot, and started an intravenous on her, all in under five minutes. But just watching them do all of it had made Jack violently nauseous. He was sitting with his eyes closed in a chair in the corner, with the room spinning around him.

"Let's get Mr. Watson a cup of coffee, black, shall we?" the doctor said, and the nurse raised an eyebrow.

"IV?"

"Good idea." The medical team chuckled, and Jack opened one eye and looked at them as Amanda suffered through the next pain, but the morphine had at least taken the edge off.

"Why is everyone so loud here?" Jack complained just as Jan and Louise walked in, and went straight to their mother.

"You shouldn't be here," she told Jan groggily. The morphine was making her sleepy.

"Why not, Mom?" She touched her cheek gently and stroked her hair, as Louise went to get her ice chips. When she was in labor, it had been all she wanted.

"Because you'll never want to have children. This is awful," and then she added as an afterthought, having closed her eyes for just a minute, "but it's worth it. I love you, baby," she whispered to her and then drifted off again, as Louise came back into the room with the ice chips. "I love you too, Louise," she said, and gratefully accepted the ice chips. Jack was still sitting in the corner, drinking coffee.

And at five o'clock, when the doctor checked her again, they decided she was ready to go to the delivery room, but the morphine was wearing off by then, and Amanda was complaining.

"I feel awful . . . why do I feel so awful . . . ?"

"Because you're having a baby," Louise told her, as Jack walked over to stand beside her. He was looking a lot more sober.

"How are you doing, sweetheart?" he asked, looking sympathetic.

"I feel awful."

"I'll bet you do." And then he looked at the nurse with annoyance. "Can't you give her something? Why don't you put her out, for chrissake?"

"Because she's having a baby, not brain surgery, and she has to push now."

"I don't want to push. I hate pushing. I hate everything. I hate this." All the morphine had done was make her feel groggy and out of it, but she still felt every pain.

"It'll be over soon," he said as he followed the gurney to the delivery room, wondering how he had gotten roped into this. He didn't want to see it, but he didn't want to leave her either. And her two daughters were following right behind him. The equipment in the room alone made him feel dizzy. They offered each of them a stool near her head, and propped her up to a nearly sitting position with her feet in stirrups, and over in the corner was a small plastic bassinet, with a heat light on it, to keep it warm for the baby. It suddenly made it all so real to him. They were here for a reason. Something great was happening. They weren't just there to watch her suffer.

But after a while, it began to feel as though that was why they had come here. She pushed for two hours and got nowhere. The baby was enormous. There were whispers among the medical team, and the doctor glanced at the clock and nodded. "We'll give her another ten minutes." But Jack was alert by now, and he had heard them.

"What does that mean?"

"The baby's not moving much, Jack," the doctor said quietly. "And Amanda's pretty tired. We may have to give her a hand here."

"What kind of a hand?" He looked panicked. He knew even before they told him. The training film. The caesarean. The one that looked liked they had cut the woman in half with the chain saw. And he looked at the doctor in open terror. "Do you have to?"

"We'll see. Maybe not, if she helps us." Amanda was miserable by then, she was crying and clutching his hands, and both her daughters looked worried. But Jack looked worse than she did. And five minutes later, there had been no improvement. They were standing around waiting for the next pain, when an alarm went off, and the entire room seemed to be filled with buzzing and everyone leaped into action around her.

"What is that? What happened?" Jack looked panicked, and totally sober.

"It's the fetal monitor, Jack. The baby's in trouble," the doctor explained, but he was too busy to say more. There were instructions flying everywhere, and the anesthesiologist was saying something to Amanda and she was crying.

"What kind of trouble?" Jack was desperate to know what was happening and no one would tell him.

"You have to leave the room now, all of you," the doctor said loudly, and then to the anesthesiologist: "Do we have time for an epidural?"

"I'll try it," he answered. More running, more instructions, noise everywhere, and Amanda reaching for Jack's hand like a wounded animal as she lay there. The girls had already left the room by then, but Jack knew he couldn't leave her. He couldn't do this to her.

"I took the class," he told anyone who would listen. "I took the Lamaze class with the film on C-sections. . . ." But no one was listening, their eyes were glued to the monitor, and they were still trying unsuccessfully to wrest his son from Amanda.

The epidural was in place by then, and the doctor looked at Jack sternly. "Sit down, and talk to her." They put a screen in front of her so he couldn't see the surgery, only her face, and the anesthesiologist seemed to be doing a thousand things at once, and there were trays of instruments being moved around as Jack tried not to watch them. But all he could see now were her eyes, her face, and the terror he saw there.

"It's all right, baby, I'm here. It's going to be fine. They'll have the baby out in a minute." He found himself silently praying that he wasn't lying to her.

"Is he okay? Is the baby okay, Jack?" She was crying and talking all at once, but she felt no pain now, just a lot of tugging and pulling. And Jack kept his eyes on her, telling her how much he loved her.

"The baby's fine," he kept telling her, willing it to be true, praying that nothing had happened to the baby. He didn't want that to happen to her. She had been through too much now. The baby had to come through it. But the surgery seemed to take forever. There was sweat falling off Jack's face onto the drape next to her, and his tears mixed with hers as they waited. There was an endless ticking in the room, and then a sudden silence as she began to cry harder.

It was as though she knew, as though she sensed that something terrible was about to happen, and all he could do was kiss her and tell her how much he loved her. But how would he ever make it up to her if the baby died? He knew that no matter what he did, he couldn't. And as he looked at her, willing their son to live, they suddenly heard a small wailing sound that filled the room, and her eyes opened wide in wonder.

"Is he okay?" She was completely worn out, but it was all she wanted to know now, and the doctor was quick to reassure her.

"He's fine." They cut the cord, and put him in the scale to weigh him as Jack went to look at his boy, his son. Nine pounds twelve ounces. Almost ten pounds. He had fought hard to get here. He had her big blue eyes, and a look of astonishment on his face as though he had arrived sooner than he meant to. And he had. He was almost three weeks early.

They cleaned him up and wrapped him in a blanket then, and lay him next to his mother, but her arms were still strapped to boards and she couldn't hold him. Jack held him for her, and his eyes filled with tears as he watched Amanda look at her son for the first time, and touch him with her cheek. Nothing had ever moved him more than this woman he had come to love so much, and the baby neither of them had expected. He was a small dream being born, a large hope for the future, a special delivery from heaven. And suddenly Jack didn't feel old, but young, as he looked down at them. It was a gift of magic for the future. Like opening a window onto sunlight.

"He's so beautiful," she whispered as she looked up at Jack. "He looks like you."

"I hope not," he said, with tears rolling down his cheeks as he bent to kiss her. "Thank you," he said to her ". . . for not giving him up . . . for wanting him when I didn't."

"I love you," she said sleepily. It was eight o'clock in the morning, and their baby was ten minutes old now.

"I love you too," he said, watching her as she drifted off to sleep, and they took the baby away to the nursery, while they finished ministering to his mother. He sat for a long time, watching her, and when they rolled her back to her room finally, after the recovery room, she was still sound asleep, and he was still with her.

The others were waiting for them there, they had already heard the news, Paul was there too, and they were all smiling.

"Congratulations!" Louise was the first to say it, and for once, she meant it.